The Turning Point

Naomi J. Karp

The Turning Point

HARCOURT BRACE JOVANOVICH

NEW YORK AND LONDON

Printed in the United States of America

First edition

B C D E F G H I J K

Library of Congress Cataloging in Publication Data

Karp, Naomi J
The turning point.

SUMMARY: A young Jewish girl encounters anti-Semitism when her family moves from the Bronx to the suburbs.

[1. Anti-Semitism—Fiction. 2. Prejudices—Fiction. 3. Family life—Fiction] I. Title.

PZ7.K148Tu   [Fic]   76-12987
ISBN 0-15-291238-X

The Turning Point

One

"YOU MAY KEES MY HAND," HANNAH SAID TO
the mirror. She lifted her chin and squinted her eyes
as she had seen Norma Shearer do in the movies as
Marie Antoinette. "Ha, ha, ha, my prince," she said,
laughing haughtily.

The Spanish shawl, draped around her shoulders,
kept slipping.

"Just a minute," she said to the mirror as she grasped
the shawl around her waist. "O.K." Then she extended
her other hand and admired herself.

If only her hair were longer, she could pile it high on
her head, and if only she didn't have to wear these
stupid eyeglasses. Hannah removed them, and the image
in the mirror became a blur, the red roses of the shawl
like big ink stains.

"Oh, it's no use," she said. She removed the shawl and
laid it back on the piano, which it had covered for as
long as she could remember. Only now that all the
family photographs had been taken off and put in boxes,
the shawl was temptingly accessible.

"Face it, Hannah, you're ugly," she whispered. But,
these days, everything was ugly. She hated living in the
apartment with boxes piled everywhere, the rugs rolled
up revealing scratched floors, and, worst of all, no cur-
tains on the windows.

"Ma," Hannah called. "Are you absolutely, positively certain that we have to move?"

"What!" Her mother called from somewhere under the kitchen sink, where she was scrubbing the pipes so that the new tenants wouldn't think she was a poor housekeeper. "Hannah, did you empty your closet?"

"It's on my bed. But where will I sleep tonight?" Under the bed, Hannah thought, walking back into her bedroom, where it will be dark and silent and where, if she stayed forever, nobody would find her. Her parents and Zack would move to the new house, and she would be left behind, oh, happily, joyously, still on Tremont Avenue in the Bronx. Perhaps the new tenants would adopt her, and when she grew up, she would take a taxi and visit her parents and Zack, who would not recognize her because she was so beautiful and rich.

Or, maybe her best friend, Shirley Levine, would smuggle in her food and homework so that she would not starve or be left back. After all, she would be entering eighth grade in September, and it would be very embarrassing to be left back.

"No chance of that," Hannah said, pushing aside the pile of clothing on the bed and lying down. She had already skipped one grade and was still the smartest in the class. Not only that, but she was two-thousand-year-old Mr. Benjamin's pet. Principal's Pet. That hadn't been easy. There was lots of competition. But Hannah had worked her way up from toilet monitor in the fifth grade (which meant that she had to make sure everybody flushed) to the one most often chosen to run down to the delicatessen for Mr. Benjamin's corned beef on rye and a cream soda.

"A lot of good it'll do me now," Hannah thought.

She would be the new girl in school, somebody unknown.

"Hey, Ma," Hannah called from her bedroom. "Do you think Mr. Benjamin will give me a letter of recommendation? Ma, do you? Oh, Ma, I thought you were in the kitchen." Hannah looked at her mother in surprise.

"Would you like me to take you by the arm, young lady, and march you into the kitchen, where you can help me put the pots and pans in a box?" Mrs. Brand waved a filthy rag at her daughter.

"That's not fair, Ma. I mean, I don't want to move, so why should I aid and abet you?"

"I'll give you aid and abet. Get off that bed and get to work. Twelve years old and lying on her bed while her mother slaves in the August heat so that she should have a better life." Mrs. Brand moved toward Hannah, but her daughter jumped up quickly.

"Nobody said you have to scrub the pipes in the kitchen, Ma. Ich, don't hit me with that dirty rag." She held up her arm to protect herself, although she knew her mother would not slap her. She never had.

"One day, Hannah, my darling, one day you will come home from school and you will find me sprawled on the floor, dead from aggravation," Mrs. Brand warned.

"Yeah, Ma, I'm sorry." Hannah bent over her kneeling mother and kissed her on the head.

"Never mind that. Don't try to *shmaichel* me," Mrs. Brand said, pushing an empty carton toward her daughter, one of dozens Hannah and Zack had carried home from the grocery store on the corner.

"What's *shmaichel*?" Hannah asked, banging pots

5

and pans into the box as fast as she could.

"Someone who tries to get on the good side of you with hugs and kisses when she really doesn't mean it."

"I mean it, Ma. I love you, honest. I just don't understand why we have to move."

"Oh, I can't stand it another minute. Do you have to bang those pans like that? It sounds like an army of madmen." Mrs. Brand held her head as if trying to keep it from falling to pieces. "Look, Hannah, do me a favor. Go out and find Shirley and your other friends and play."

"No, I want to help," Hannah said, trying to jam an iron frying pan into the already full box.

"Please. Go."

"Well, if you really want me to," Hannah said. Without wasting a moment, she raced out the door, slamming it noisily behind her.

She knew where Shirley would be, where she always was these days. Hannah sighed as she remembered the good old days that had lasted until about three weeks ago. In those days, she and Shirley had roller-skated through the entire neighborhood. They had challenged the kids in the next apartment house to a jacks tournament and had won. Nobody could jump rope like Shirley—even Hannah admitted that—and they had spent the long evenings of June and July swinging their ropes until old Mrs. Greenspan had complained to Shirley's mother that they had whipped the newspaper right out of her hands while she was sitting in front of the building.

But these last three weeks Shirley had turned into a mope. Whenever she saw Hannah, she would burst into tears and turn away. And whenever Hannah called for her to come and play, she would say that she was busy. "Doing what?" Hannah asked. "Sewing?"

"Sewing!" Hannah said as she pushed open Shirley's door. She could hear the hum of Mrs. Levine's old machine and the pump, pump as Shirley pushed the pedal that made it go. "Hey, Shoiley," Hannah yelled, imitating her friend's mother. "Watcha doin'?"

A chair scraped and then a door slammed. Shirley stood there, her long brown curls stuck to her neck with perspiration. She glanced behind her as if to make sure Hannah couldn't see into the bedroom where the sewing machine stood. "Oh, hi!"

"Come on out," Hannah said. "How can you stay in here? It's so hot."

"I hadn't noticed," Shirley said, patting her forehead with one of her many handkerchiefs embroidered by her very own hand, as her mother liked to say. "I'm busy."

Shirley wasn't crying this time, or at least it was hard for Hannah to tell if the dampness on her face was tears or perspiration.

"Well, tomorrow's the day," Hannah said. "I thought we could share one last moment together."

Shirley took a deep breath. "Oh, Hannah, you're mean. Why did you have to remind me?" She blew her nose loudly, and Hannah wondered if the elaborate stitches on the handkerchief scratched her nose.

"Well, I haven't seen you blubbering for at least twenty-four hours. Come on, Shirley, I was only kidding. Don't cry. It's not as if I died or something." Shirley's tears made Hannah uncomfortable. She wished she could cry, too, but she never did. Except once, in the movies, when a horse broke his leg and they had to shoot him. Now, that was sad. Perhaps, if she thought of that scene now, it would make her cry. Hannah concentrated on the movie, but it didn't work.

"You may as well d . . . pass away. I probably will never see you again." Shirley sobbed. "Relatives of ours moved to the country, somewhere near where you're going, and nobody ever heard from them again. Their name was Shapiro."

"Are you kidding? Of course, you'll see me again. I'll come here and you'll come there practically all the time. No, let's make it definite. I want you to come for Christmas vacation. That's only"—Hannah counted the months on her fingers—"four months or so."

"That's ages and ages." Shirley sniffed.

"Anyway, you're the lucky one," Hannah said. "You get to stay here with all the kids. I . . ." She took a deep breath and stared out the window, hoping she looked like Bette Davis courageously saying farewell to Errol Flynn. "While I must go out into a world of strangers, unknown and unloved."

At once, Shirley rushed across the room and threw her arms around Hannah. "That's terrible. I never thought of that."

"Come on, let's get out of here. I know. Let's go downstairs and shave Eli Maxwell's mustache off. He's probably sleeping on the stairs, poor fat slob."

Shirley laughed. "Hannah, you're absolutely horrible."

"Good. That means you'll be better off without me."

"Don't ever say that, Hannah," Shirley said, taking her friend by the shoulders. "You are my one and only truest, bestest friend in the whole world."

"So, let's get your father's razor and we'll get started on Eli," Hannah said quickly, for it looked as though

Shirley was about to start weeping again. And it almost worked. Shirley smiled, but then turned back to the bedroom, slamming the door behind her. Hannah could hear her sobs mixed in with the hum of the sewing machine.

"Don't drop tears on the material," she called. "It might shrink." But she knew Shirley couldn't hear her.

TWO

MR. BRAND WAS OBVIOUSLY EMBARRASSED.
For one thing, he couldn't remember the names of all
his neighbors, people he had lived next door to for many
years. And now, when he would never see them again,
he was trying very hard to sort them out.

"It was wonderful knowing you, Mr. Blupblup," he
mumbled to a man who was shaking his hand as if it
were a pump. "Thank you for your good wishes, Esther
. . . I mean, Zelda. No, I will never forget the good
times we had here. They were good years, yes." He
turned to his wife who was directing the moving men
as if she were a sergeant in the army. "Lillie, who are
all these people?" he whispered.

"If you didn't keep your head in your books night
and day, maybe you would have met a few," Mrs. Brand
said, still pointing out pieces of furniture to the movers.
"That's it," she shouted to the men. "The rest we take
in the car. Zachary, make sure that rope is tight." She
gave her son a small push toward the car, and Zack
tested the rope and the suitcases it held atop the car
roof.

"We look like gypsies," he said to Hannah.

"Are you going to hold your basketball all the way to
your new house?" Hannah asked him.

"Do you think I would trust my prize possession on a strange truck?"

"All right, children, let's go," Mrs. Brand called. "Hannah, you can sit on top of the winter coats in the back seat. Zack, squeeze up front between Daddy and me." She turned and waved, but Mrs. Levine grabbed her.

"Lillie, good luck. May God be with you. Here." She shoved an enormous cake box into Mrs. Brand's hands. "Something sweet for your new home."

"Where's Shirley?" Hannah asked Mrs. Levine. "I didn't say good-by to her."

"Don't worry, she's coming. Look, here she is. Come, Shoiley, did you finish it?"

Silently, Shirley handed Hannah a brown paper bag. "For you to remember me by," she whispered. "That's what I was sewing all this week."

"Hey, thanks, Shirl," Hannah said, wondering if she should take out whatever was in the bag. If it was a slip or underwear, she would faint. "What is it?" she whispered.

"Open it and see."

Hannah turned away from the group and dug her hand into the bag. Embroidery, she definitely felt that.

"Oh, how lovely," Mrs. Brand said, "a dresser scarf." She was trying to hurry Hannah along and made the announcement so that Hannah would not have to show everybody the gift.

"It's swell, Shirl. Thanks a lot," Hannah said, stuffing it back in the bag, but Shirley pulled it out again.

"I embroidered something on it. A poem I made up."

Hannah squinted at the tiny stitches around the edges. "When you dress up like a queen, remember Shirley Levine. August 1938," she read. Hannah squeezed Shirley's arm and kissed her quickly on the cheek. "Thanks a lot. I'll write," she called as her mother pulled her toward the car.

"Good-by, everybody," Mrs. Brand shouted and then turned to her husband. "Let's go, Dave. I'm either going to faint or cry or both. Oi, are you going to smoke that smelly cigar?"

Finally, Mr. Brand pulled the car away from the curb. Mrs. Brand waved to the moving truck to follow them, and Hannah got a last glimpse of Shirley, who was crying on her mother's shoulder.

"Well, a new adventure. Dave, don't go too fast. I don't want the movers to lose us."

Mr. Brand didn't answer. Instead, he hummed a monotonous little tune, his "di-diddely-dum driving song," Zack called it. "We did the right thing, Lillie," he said, after a while.

"Are you asking me or telling me?" Mrs. Brand said. "Of course we did the right thing. We must grab our opportunities, David. Remember, children, what I'm telling you. Grab your opportunities." She tried to turn around to Hannah, but the front seat was too crowded.

"The thought for the day," Hannah mumbled. "What kind of opportunity did you grab, Ma?" she asked, louder.

"Fresh air for my children, no more Zack playing ball in the street, where, God forbid, he would be run over by a truck. A home of our own. Thank heavens, your father, may he live and be well, has prospered in his business, although I never will know why, with his head stuck in a book night and day, so that he can afford to give us a better life."

"Is that all one sentence?" Hannah asked.

"Never mind, my smart-mouthed daughter," Mrs. Brand said, making a major effort to face her daughter and almost pushing Zack into his father's lap. "That is another thing. Maybe, away from those fresh kids, you'll learn how to be a lady."

"Shirley's not a fresh kid," Hannah said.

"I'm not talking about Shirley. She's the only decent one."

"Who, then?"

"You know who I mean. That Howard, for one."

"Howie?" Zack asked. "He's not Hannah's friend. He's mine."

Mrs. Brand ignored him. "Like roses in a garbage can. That's how my children were there."

Hannah giggled and poked Zack on the back of his head. "Hey, rose," she said, laughing. She could see his black curly hair bounce up and down as he tried to hide his own laughter.

Hannah sat back on the pile of clothing, her head touching the ceiling of the car whenever they went over a bump. It was amazing, she thought, how her father knew exactly where to turn, what streets to go up, which bridge to go over. For someone who didn't seem to pay attention to the world around him, he knew quite a bit.

"Are we almost there?" she asked, coughing loudly. Her father's cigar smelled terrible in the hot car, but at least it was better than in winter when her mother made sure all the windows were cranked up tight. Hannah wished she had gone to see the house before, but she had refused to show any interest in it. She didn't want to live anywhere else but on Tremont Avenue with friends she had grown up with and where she knew what to expect. She didn't like surprises, especially when everyone else knew something she didn't. That was why she had been so annoyed at her eleventh birthday party when she had walked into a darkened living room after returning from the movies to hear whispers and giggles and then suddenly a shout of "Surprise!" Hannah had glared angrily at her parents and then at Shirley for keeping this secret from her. Everyone had thought she was just so surprised that she could barely speak for the entire afternoon and that the day had been a great success. Little did they know, Hannah thought.

Now she wished she had gone with her parents and Zack on one of their visits to "look over the property," as her father called it.

"Is this it?" Hannah asked as they passed a street sign that said "Dudley Road." Her father pulled the car into a narrow driveway. The moving truck rumbled and squeaked behind them as it stopped. She got out of the car, as the rest of the family did, and examined their new home, a neat white house with a front porch and a large tree whose leaves swept the top of the car. "It's pretty nice," she said reluctantly.

Mr. Brand looked at her happily while he wiped his face with his handkerchief, carefully avoiding the tiny stub of cigar in his mouth. Then he removed it, searched around for a place to discard it, and, testing the end to see if it was cold, stuffed it in his pocket. "I don't want to make it dirty," he said, pointing to the driveway.

Zack stretched and bent, trying to relieve his cramped body until Mrs. Brand announced, "All right, everybody. Let's get to work."

Zack grabbed hold of a large carton with one hand while refusing to let go of the basketball still tucked under his arm. Hannah watched him struggle for a moment, then moved to help him as she saw they had an audience.

"Look," she said, pointing to a small group of children across the street. They were watching, silently, some waving to the burly moving men, who ignored them.

"Little kids," Zack said, and pretended to throw his ball to them. They giggled and moved backward.

"Never mind the welcoming committee," Mrs. Brand said. "Hannah, take in the clothes on the back seat. David, what are you doing?" She stopped and watched her husband pull a small hammer from his pocket and carefully nail a silver *mezuzah* to the front doorpost.

"Now God knows that a Jewish family lives here," he said. He kissed his fingertips and then touched them to the small symbol. "As it is said in Deuteronomy, we shall remember God's commandments and write them upon the doorposts of our house and upon our gates."

Three

"I CAN'T," ZACK SAID, PUSHING ASIDE THE plate of toast. "I've got to run." He jumped up from the table, ran his fingers through his hair as if they were a comb, and disappeared.

Hannah watched him go, almost tempted to run after him. But she had done that once before this week, following her brother to the schoolyard, where he had found a pickup basketball game. She had stared through the rusted wrought-iron fence, listening to the shouting boys who already knew her brother's name.

"Here, Zack, throw it here. I'm free," or, "That was a good layup shot, Zack." They would poke each other and tie handkerchiefs around their foreheads to keep the perspiration from their eyes.

But, after a while, when nobody paid any attention to her, she walked back to the house. Why couldn't she be like him, she had thought. Zack made friends wherever he went. Even on the subway when they would be going to a museum or to visit their grandparents, Zack would find something to talk about with the person sitting next to him. Old ladies with shopping bags would tell him about bargains they had found; neatly dressed men with briefcases would give him advice on a business he should go into when he was older; even little kids, sitting on their mothers' laps, would smile at him shyly and then ask to sit on his lap. By the time they got off the train, these people would nod and wave to Zack as if he were their long-lost relative.

"So, Miss Grump, why are you sitting here? Go outside in the sunshine and find somebody to play with, also," her mother said. "You look like a ghost wandering around the house."

"Aw, leave me alone, Ma," Hannah mumbled. But she picked up a book and went outside to sit on the porch steps, biting her lip and feeling sorry for herself. She closed her eyes and lifted her face toward the warm sun. It felt good, but she tried not to let her unhappiness slip away from her. If she did, Hannah decided, she would be disloyal. To the Bronx, to her old friends, and, most important, to herself. She would not give in.

She would let everyone know how miserable she was. She would punish her parents for taking her away against her will.

Like being in captivity, Hannah thought, pretending she was on a large ship in the middle of the ocean. She was standing on the deck, looking sadly off into the distance, her long hair flying in the wind.

"Farewell, native land. I shall never see you again," she mumbled. Ah, if they would only remove these shackles from her ankles so that she could jump overboard and swim back. There, Shirley would be waiting for her on the dock, waving one of her dumb handkerchiefs. "Ah, woe, ah, misery," she said, squeezing her eyes so that tears might come.

"Who you talking to?" a voice asked.

Hannah sat up straight, startled. She tried to open her eyes, but the sun was too strong. She moved up one step into the shade of the porch. Before her stood a tall girl with very red hair. Her legs and her face were smothered in freckles. "None of your business," Hannah said.

The girl ignored Hannah's rudeness and asked, "What's your name?"

"What's yours?" Hannah asked, unwilling to reveal her identity to a total stranger.

"Cynthia Eloise Sherwood. I live over there, across the street."

"Oh." Hannah looked at the house Cynthia had nodded toward. "Well, I guess I can tell you. Hannah" —she stopped, searching for a middle name that would be as fancy as Cynthia's—"Hannah Deanna Brand."

"Like Deanna Durbin in the movies?" Cynthia asked.

"Yeah, but I had it first. She copied me."

"I don't believe you. She probably doesn't even know who you are." Cynthia pouted.

Hannah shrugged and partly lowered her eyelids to make her look more mysterious. But it was hard to look mysterious when you wore glasses, she supposed; at least, Cynthia didn't seem impressed.

"Are you the only kid on the block?" Hannah asked. "I mean, beside all those kindergarten kids?"

"No, but you wouldn't like the others."

"Why not? What's wrong with them? Where are they, anyhow?" Hannah leaned forward and looked down the street as if expecting to see doors fly open and people appear, kicking their legs and doing a tap dance, the way they did in the movies.

"They'll be back soon. Some of them went away for the summer," Cynthia said, answering only the last of Hannah's questions.

"Well, why wouldn't I like them?" Hannah repeated.

"Oh, they're sort of—well, you know—common." Cynthia gave Hannah a small smile. "All except Arthur.

He lives next door to you. Did you meet him? He's in our class." She stopped. "What class are you in?"

"Eighth. I skipped a year," Hannah said.

"Me too. In eighth, I mean. Not skipped."

"Yeah, Cynthia, but what do you mean 'common'? What's common?" Hannah had heard her mother use that word when she mentioned neighbors who fought a lot and used bad language.

"They're just not our type," Cynthia said, growing red in the face as if the explanation was hard work.

"Oh," Hannah said. Then she asked, "Well, how do you know what type I am? How do you know I'm not common? After all, you just met me." Hannah was enjoying watching Cynthia's discomfort. "As a matter of fact, I don't even belong here," Hannah said, examining her fingernails. "I was brought here against my will. Kidnapped." She glanced up to see if Cynthia believed this.

"Humph," Cynthia snorted.

"It's true," Hannah protested. "My real home is a kingdom far across the sea. These people"—she turned her head toward her front door—"robbed me from the cradle in my palace nursery and brought me to this town. What's the name of it, again?" She looked at Cynthia helplessly.

"Hazelton. I've lived here practically all my life," Cynthia said, as if Hannah were forcing her to play this game against her will.

"So, I think it was very smart of you to see that I am not a common person like the others, whoever they are." Hannah sighed. Why had she wasted that terrific story on Cynthia, she wondered, who apparently did not have Hannah's wonderful sense of humor?

"Anyhow . . ." Cynthia said, then suddenly turned

away from Hannah and toward the house on the other side of the driveway. "Hellooo, Mrs. Marshall," she called to a woman who was coming down the walk. "My mother says thank you for the recipe. It was very good."

The woman, thin and well dressed, Hannah could see, wearing white lace gloves and a tiny flowered hat, nodded. She glanced at Hannah, but said nothing, and continued walking past the two girls toward Merrick Road.

"That's Mrs. Marshall," Cynthia said. "Arthur's mother. Isn't she beautiful?"

"Doesn't she speak English?" Hannah asked.

Cynthia looked shocked. "Of course she speaks English. They're Yankees. Arthur's great-great-great-great-grandfather fought in the Revolutionary War." She was counting on her fingers to see if she had put in enough "greats."

"You mean 'Yenkees.'" Hannah laughed. "That's what my grandmother calls practically anybody who doesn't speak with an accent. She and my grandfather have this hardware store in the city, and anyone, even if they're Polish or Irish, as long as they don't speak with an accent, my grandma calls them Yenkees." She poked Cynthia, inviting her in on the joke.

But Cynthia wasn't laughing. "Oh," she said in a small voice. "I didn't know."

"How could you know my grandma?" Hannah asked. "She hasn't visited us yet."

"No, that isn't what I didn't know," Cynthia said slowly. "Listen, I have to go now. See you around."

"Hey," Hannah called. "Why? You didn't tell me about the other kids yet. Come on in and my mother

will give us some cupcakes or something." She was still
shouting when Cynthia walked into her own house.
"What's the matter with her?" Hannah asked aloud.
"Hey, Ma, listen to what just happened," Hannah called
as she went back into the house. It would be even more
proof that they shouldn't have moved to this crazy place.

Four

THEY APPROACHED THROUGH THE BACK-
yard gate like a small, straggling army. Hannah watched
them through the kitchen window.

"Hey, Ma, some kids are using our backyard as a
shortcut. The nerve!"

"They shouldn't step on the flower bed," Mrs. Brand
said as she looked over Hannah's shoulder. "That little
fellow's pants are almost falling down."

Hannah went out the back door and stood with her
arms folded, blocking the path. "No trespassing. This is
private property," she announced.

"Wah-ah-ah." The little boy wailed, and the girl who
held his hand gave it a sharp yank.

"Quit it, Teddy." She pulled a large, rumpled handkerchief from her dress pocket and swiped at his nose.

"I said you can't go through here," Hannah repeated.

"We're not going through. We're coming here." A
girl with enormous brown eyes that exactly matched the
color of her hair said, "We're coming to see you, if
you're Hannah. Are you?"

"What if I am?" Hannah asked.

"We came to say hello. We live around here," the
brown-eyed girl said sweetly.

Hannah looked the group over. Four girls about her
own age, two of them exactly alike with short braids

tied with ribbons, one set green and the other yellow, and a fat, red-nosed girl, obviously the sister of Teddy. A fifth girl, this one a few years younger, was trying to push her way toward the front.

"The common people," Hannah mumbled.

"I'm Ruth," the brown-eyed girl said. "These are the Kaplan twins, Reva and Carol, and this is Bernice and her brother, Teddy."

"How about me?" whined the youngest girl. "Tell her I'm Debbie, your sister."

Ruth sighed. "This is my sister, Debbie, who should be home playing with her own friends." She glared at Debbie, but the little girl paid no attention.

"Our mother said we should come over," Debbie said, and immediately received a hard push from Ruth.

"I told you not to say that," she hissed.

"It's O.K. I don't mind if your mother said that," Hannah said, shrugging her shoulders.

"Don't say that!" Ruth hissed again, but this time at Hannah.

"Why not?"

"Come over here and I'll tell you," she said, pulling Hannah away from the group. "Because," she whispered, "their mother died last winter, and they cry whenever they hear that word." She nodded toward Bernice and Teddy. "Don't ever say 'mother' in front of them."

"Sure," Hannah said, nodding her head.

"Who is it, Hannah? Did they step on my flowers?" Mrs. Brand called from the kitchen window.

"Some kids that came to see me," Hannah called over her shoulder. "Kids, this is my mo . . ." She looked at Bernice and Teddy and thought hard. "This is Mrs. Brand, my father's wife."

"Your father's wife?" Mrs. Brand called from the window. "What kind of thing is that to say? Just a minute." She emerged from the house with a large paper bag. "Let me look at you, children. Would you like a cookie?" She held out the bag. "No, little boy, don't put your fingers in the bag. Let me get one for you," she said as she saw Teddy wipe his nose with the back of his hand.

They stood and munched on the cookies, silently, until Hannah suggested they move to the front porch where they could sit on the steps.

"We didn't get our porch furniture yet," she explained. "My grandpa is giving us some old rockers from his cellar."

They sat on the steps, all facing the same direction, toward the street.

"See that house?" Hannah pointed to where Cynthia lived. "I met the girl who lives there."

"You mean Cynthia Eloise Sherwood?" the green-ribboned twin asked with a mouth she made into a tight little circle. "We hate her."

"Don't say 'hate,'" Bernice said. "God will punish you if you hate anybody."

"Well, I dislike her intensely," the twin explained. "She thinks she's so great."

"Right, Reva," the other twin agreed.

Green equals Reva, yellow is Carol, Hannah tried to remember. She hoped they always wore the same ribbons.

"You're not in the same class with her," Ruth told the twins. "You don't know what a teacher's pet she tries to be. They're in seventh." She pointed to the twins. "We're in eighth." She tapped her own chest and then Bernice's.

"Me, too, in eighth," Hannah said, feeling strangely happy and at home.

"We just came back from the country," Debbie said. "We stayed at a hotel that has a big lake and boats."

"Only for two weeks," Ruth added. "It costs a lot to stay all summer."

"Do you go away?" Carol asked Hannah. "Reva and I were at camp. We go every year—"

"—to the same camp," Carol finished.

"Hail to thee, Camp Winneshewauka, Nestled in the Silver Lakes," they sang together.

"No," Hannah said when they had finished their song, "this summer we spent. . . . Well, the first part was swell." She told them about Shirley and the jacks tournament and roller skating. They asked her to tell them about the Bronx and the apartment, and Hannah was delighted when they laughed at her story about how Shirley whipped the newspaper out of Mrs. Greenspan's hands with the jump rope.

"What about the second part?" Reva asked.

"Ooh, that was the icky part. My mother and father bought this house, and we had to pack. What a mess!"

"She said 'mother,' " Teddy wailed.

"Oh, I'm sorry. I forgot. I mean my parents. Is that O.K.?" she asked Ruth.

"Is that O.K., Bernice? Can we say parents?" Ruth asked.

Bernice heaved her shoulders and shook her head.

Hannah wondered how many different ways she could mention her mother without saying the word. "My grandma's daughter or my Aunt Stella's sister" were all she could think of. Maybe she could just call her Lillie.

"Shirley sounds nice," Reva said. "Is she coming to visit you?"

"Maybe," Hannah said slowly. Earlier in the week, that was all she could think of—having Shirley come and visit. Now, meeting all these swell kids. . . . She looked at them with sudden affection. Hazelton might not be so bad, after all. "If she ever stops crying." Hannah laughed. "Do you know what she was doing the last time I saw her?"

"What?" everybody asked eagerly.

"She was standing on the sidewalk bawling her eyes out on her mother's shoulder. Oh!" She clapped her hand over her mouth. "I mean . . ." But it was too late. Bernice had begun to sob loudly, rocking back and forth on the step, and Teddy, burying his face in her lap, joined her.

"For Pete's sake," Hannah said, giving them both a look of disgust. "I'm sorry, Bernice. I'm sorry. I thought it was only my mother I couldn't talk about. You don't even know Shirley's mother."

The other girls had leaned toward Bernice and were patting her on the shoulder. Hannah watched them helplessly.

"I said I was sorry," she repeated, beginning to get angry.

"Well, you didn't have to keep saying that word over and over," Ruth whispered. "Now look what you've done."

Hannah stood up and put her hands on her hips. "Listen, if she died last winter, don't you think it's about time they got over it?"

There was a gasp and then silence. Finally, Ruth stood, too, and glared at Hannah. "Well, I never! Don't you think you would cry if your mother died?" she said.

"I guess," Hannah admitted, then added, "but not

forever." She could not imagine her mother dead, so this was easy enough to say.

"Well, I'll never stop crying," Bernice shouted. "I loved my mother very much." She clutched her dirty little brother to her. "Come on, Teddy, let's go home. Hannah, I wish you never moved here. I—I hate you."

"You mean you dislike me intensely," Hannah said in a low voice.

Ruth, the twins, and Debbie rose also, seemingly undecided about what to do.

"We better go," Ruth said, finally. "I'm sure you didn't mean what you said, Hannah. Maybe you should apologize again to Bernice." She smiled.

Hannah was tempted. Ruth seemed as if she really wanted everyone to be friends. But then she heard her own voice saying, "Don't tell me what to do. I didn't invite you here. I didn't ask that girl to slobber all over my front porch. Go home, if you want. I don't care." She turned quickly, almost tripping up the steps, and slammed the screen door as hard as she could.

"Where are your new little friends?" Mrs. Brand asked as Hannah stormed into the kitchen. "I thought they might like some lemonade."

"They left," Hannah said, and much to her own and her mother's surprise, she threw her arms around her mother's waist and hugged her.

Five

"HEY, WATCHA DOING?" HANNAH CALLED from the front porch.

The boy had rolled a bicycle out onto the grass in front of his house and was carefully taking it apart.

"Are you Arthur?" Hannah asked.

He looked up, but said nothing.

Hannah walked toward him, careful to stop at the edge of the driveway that divided the Brands' property from their neighbors', the Marshalls.

"Boy, I hope you can get it all together again. It looks like a swell bike." She watched him loosen bolts and lay them in a neat row.

"Get out of here," the boy said. "I'm busy."

"Well, I know people who can work and talk at the same time. There's a man in my father's factory who makes up poems while he runs a big machine. And he never makes a mistake."

"Who cares?" Arthur sneered. "Scram!"

"His name is Mr. Bellini. My father says that's a nice name for a poet."

"Listen," the boy said, picking up a wrench. "I said scram. I don't want to hear about Mr. Bellini or any other foreigners."

"Foreigners? Mr. Bellini lives in Brooklyn. He's American, like you and me," Hannah explained.

"Maybe like you, but not like me," the boy said. "Now, s-c-r-a-m!"

"Hey, you can spell. That's good, because I hear we're in the same class." Hannah made a face at him, but he wasn't looking at her. "School starts tomorrow."

"No kidding. Boy, you must be a brain to know that."

"Hey, Arthur," Hannah whispered.

"What?"

"Nothing. I just wanted to see if that was your name."

"You see this?" Arthur said, waving the wrench. "It's going to land right on your fat head if you don't go away."

"You can't make me. I'm on my own property. See?" She pointed to her feet.

"Well, your smell is coming on to my property." Arthur snickered and held his nose.

"I don't smell. I take a bath every day," Hannah said angrily. She took a few steps backward and looked around, hoping her mother would call her so that she could get away without seeming to surrender.

"It's a smell you're born with. You never lose it," Arthur said. "What's your name?"

Hannah was startled. She didn't think he would be interested. She told him.

"Look, Hannah Brand, why don't you and your smell disappear? Scram."

"Them's fightin' words, pardner," said a low voice behind Hannah.

She whirled and faced her brother, who was standing in the shadow of the porch, almost unseen. He leaned against the porch railing and chewed on a piece of grass. Next to him was another boy doing the same thing. But while Zack looked like the cowboy he was imitating, tall, thin, and relaxed, the other boy looked ridiculous. More like the horse, Hannah thought.

"Me and mah new friend, Irwin, here, we don't like that kind o' talk, specially to a lady. Do we, Irwin?" Zack asked, narrowing his eyes at Arthur.

Irwin shook his round head. His round body was already shaking with laughter. He obviously thought Zack was hilarious.

"Well," Arthur whined as tall Zack and lumbering Irwin came out of the shadows, "she was bothering me."

"She?" Zack bellowed. "We refer to cats as she. This lady has a name, buster."

"Hannah," Arthur said quickly. "Hannah was bothering me."

"Well now, that's better. Exactly how was my sister, Hannah, bothering you?"

"She was talking to me while I was trying to fix my bike," Arthur said, looking toward Zack for sympathy.

"Talking to you, was she? Hear that, Irwin? My sister, Hannah, was talking to this young fellow while he was trying to fix his bike. I declare, young fellow, you had every right to instruct Hannah to leave."

"What?" Hannah shrieked. "Whose side are you on, anyway?"

"He did say to you, Hannah, did he not, to kindly remove yourself from his presence as your dazzling beauty was distracting him? Did he not?"

"He told me to scram because I smelled bad."

"Yes, I seem to have heard that part. How about you, Irwin?"

Irwin nodded, wiping tears of laughter from his eyes.

"Then there is only one way I can preserve the honor of my family," Zack said softly. "Apologize, you cad!"

he shouted at Arthur, darting his hand quickly toward the boy and grabbing him by the arm.

"Let go, you're hurting me," Arthur whined.

"Apologize." Zack was insistent.

With a sudden movement, Arthur pulled loose and ran toward his front door.

"The lad is obviously no gentleman," Zack said with a sigh. "What's more, he's a coward, picking on a poor, innocent little girl."

"Quit it," Hannah said.

"You keep away from me," Arthur shouted, one hand on his front doorknob. "Just keep your dirty hands off me, you—you—Christ-killers!" He opened his door and disappeared.

Zack, Hannah, and Irwin froze where they stood. Hannah could her her brother breathing very hard, and Irwin was making a low, growling sound.

"Why, that little Nazi," Zack said at last. "I'm going in there and pull him out. I'm going to take that ugly little face and push it—"

"Ah, Zack, you know better than that," Irwin said soothingly. "He's not worth it. He's only a dumb kid."

"Dumb kid! That's what they said about Hitler and his gang, at first. Now look at them. No, I'm not going to let him get away with it, Irwin."

"No!" Hannah shouted as her brother moved toward the Marshall house. "Don't, please, Zack. Maybe it was my fault. I shouldn't have kept talking to him. It was my fault. Don't go in there." She grabbed hold of his shirt and pulled at it.

Zack stopped and looked at Hannah. "O.K., just this time. But, if he ever . . ." He made a fist and socked it hard into the palm of his other hand.

31

"What a place," Hannah mumbled.

"Oh, it's not so bad," Irwin said. "It's just like any other place."

"It's not like the Bronx," Hannah said.

Irwin smiled. "You just didn't come across it there," he said. "It's that way all over the world."

Six

———◆◆◆———

"YOU HAVE ONLY YOURSELF TO BLAME," Mrs. Brand said. "Why did you have to go butt in?" She shook her finger at Hannah.

"Zack was right. I shouldn't have told you," Hannah said, angry at herself as well as her mother.

"What you told us, Hannah, my darling, was an old, old story," Mr. Brand said, without looking up from his newspaper. "I'm thankful it didn't happen to you sooner, that's all."

"But you don't understand," Hannah whined. "We're living next door to Nazis."

"Don't be ridiculous," her father said. "Just because that foolish boy called you a—a—name doesn't mean they're Nazis." He shrugged. "Ignorant, that's all. Now, don't think about it anymore." He patted Hannah's hand and went back to reading his newspaper.

"O-o-oh, where's Zack? Why isn't he here to tell you what happened?" Hannah asked the air.

"Never mind Zack. He's a smart boy, and he knows what I'm telling you is right," Mr. Brand said impatiently. He did not like to be interrupted at his reading.

"Just keep away from him, that boy next door. Don't talk to him. Don't look at him. Just keep away," Mrs. Brand said.

"He's in my class," Hannah shouted. "How can I keep away from him?"

"Easy," her mother said. "If he sits in the back row, you sit in the front. If he walks on this side of the street, you walk on the other."

"But why should I get out of his way? Why shouldn't he get out of mine?" Hannah asked. What was the matter with her parents? she wondered. Were they afraid of something? "He's the one who did something wrong."

"Because," her father said, finally looking up from his paper, "that's the way it is."

Hannah looked at her father. He didn't usually use that tone of voice.

"Oh, O.K.," she said between her teeth and walked angrily out of the room.

She stood at her bedroom window and looked down at the street. There were lights on in Cynthia's house across the road, and she could see the red-haired girl whenever she moved in front of the living-room window.

"She thinks the Marshalls are so great," Hannah thought. "I wonder if she knows—"

"Hannah," Mrs. Brand called from downstairs, "put out your blue dress and polish your shoes. Tomorrow is the first day of school. Hannah, you hear me?"

"Yeah, Ma," Hannah called. Some first day of school, she thought. Nobody to walk with. Nobody's going to talk to me. She punched the windowsill. "Ow," she said aloud. "What's wrong with me?" She had not made a single friend in the few weeks they had lived in Hazelton. Not only that, Hannah thought, she had made enemies. Cynthia was one. Hannah couldn't figure that out. Ruth and Bernice were two more. She shook her head.

Maybe she could understand that. And, Arthur. Well, that was different.

"You know what I'm going to do?" Hannah said to her mirror. "I'm going to start all over again."

"You're what?" she asked as if she were the mirror.

"I've definitely made up my mind. I'm going to be nice and sweet and maybe I'll even apologize to Bernice."

"No, don't do that. She doesn't deserve it."

"Listen," Hannah said, wagging her finger at the image in the mirror. "I'm sick of your terrible advice. Let me try it and see how it works out."

She watched herself shrug and then smile, a phony, close-lipped smile. "If it doesn't work, then I'll know it's them and not me," she whispered.

But as she turned away from the mirror and opened her closet door, she suddenly froze. The first day of school, she thought with a little shudder. How great it was in the old days, she and Shirley walking there together in their new school clothes and being greeted by the same familiar faces, knowing exactly what to expect. This year, for instance, she would have had Mrs. Brennan, who had taught the eighth grade since she could remember.

"She's tough, but fair," Zack had told her. "And she tells the same stories about her grandson to every class she ever had. The kid must be fifty by now," her brother had joked.

Well, Hannah thought, she would never hear those stories, never see Mrs. Brennan or those other familiar faces. She was entering a world of strangers, most of whom didn't even know she existed. She wondered if the teachers at Spring Street School knew that she was coming. What if her records had gotten lost in the mail? What if there was no room for her in the class? What if, when she showed up tomorrow, they would tell her they didn't believe in skipping at their school, and she would have to repeat the seventh grade?

"What if . . . what if . . ." she muttered to herself, trying to anticipate all the terrible things that could happen on that first day. She took a deep breath and rummaged around on the bottom of her closet for her school shoes, which were almost new.

"They don't need polish," she told herself. "Ma!" she shouted, "they don't need polish." But she found herself rubbing the tops of them with the hem of her bathrobe until they shone.

Seven

***

"LOOK UPON IT AS A CHALLENGE," ZACK told Hannah as he watched her stare into her cereal bowl. "You can start all over again. Be a new person. Forget your past and go on." He patted her on the shoulder and winked at Irwin, who was tapping his foot impatiently and looking at the clock above the kitchen sink.

"Come on, Zack. We'll miss the bus," he said.

"That's easy for you to say," Hannah mumbled grumpily. "You already have a friend." She pointed her spoon at Irwin. "He can show you around. You're not going into a new school alone."

"Don't be silly, Hannah. With your charming personality, you'll be head of the class in no time," Irwin said as he pulled Zack's arm. "Let's go."

Hannah watched them leave and with a deep sigh pushed herself away from the table. "I'm not hungry, Ma."

"All right," Mrs. Brand said. "Go to school on an empty stomach. Faint with hunger on your first day." She looked around the kitchen and grabbed a piece of toast from the plate. "Here, take this. Munch on your way. At least it will be something."

Reluctantly, Hannah took the bread from her mother and gave her a quick kiss on the cheek.

"You'll do fine," Mrs. Brand said. "Look, I'm putting some pennies in the *pushka* for good luck." She dropped some coins into a small blue and white box on the counter and shook it.

"What good will that do?" Hannah asked.

"Charity is one of God's commandments," Mrs. Brand said. "It couldn't hurt. When we give to others, maybe God will help us, too."

Hannah glanced at the charity box and shrugged. "If you say so," she said to her mother.

She walked quickly, afraid to be late. A new life, Zack had said. Of course, he had been kidding, but it was a good idea. Too bad she had had already met Ruth and Bernice and the others and had told them about the Bronx and all that. Otherwise, she could be the mysterious stranger, the runaway princess, hiding out in Hazelton and just pretending to be like the others. But, little by little, her background would be revealed, her foreign accent would slip out with certain words, someone would notice that the small ring on her finger was not a gift from her parents on her tenth birthday, but the seal of her kingdom, coveted by the wicked prime minister. The engraved initials, H.B., did not stand for Hannah Brand, but for . . . Hannah thought hard . . . for Her Beautiness.

She jumped when she heard a bell ring and raced for the schoolyard where the pupils of the Spring Street School were lining up to enter the building. Hannah searched for Ruth and Bernice, and when she saw them, tagged on to their line. She was still out of breath as the class shuffled through the hall, up the stairs, and into a room.

"Sit here, sit here," two girls were shouting at each

other and pointing excitedly at desks. One girl slid into a seat at the same moment that Arthur did, and with a sudden hard push, he knocked her to the floor.

"Scram, Consuelo. This is my seat," he said.

Slowly, the girl rose and brushed off her dress. "Arthur Marshall, you are the meanest person in the world," she said.

He ignored her and crumpled a piece of paper into a ball. "Catch," he yelled at a tall boy seated in the back row. "Hey, Billy, catch."

Hannah was not sure what to do. There were a few empty desks, but if someone came in late and told her to get up, that it was his seat, she would be embarrassed.

But she was embarrassed right now as the only person standing, although most of the class was so busy talking to one other and moving from seat to seat, they didn't seem to notice her.

Where was the teacher or somebody? Hannah wondered. She could feel her face getting warm, and she longed to sit down. She glanced at Ruth, who was spitting on her finger and trying to rub a large ink stain off her desk. Bernice was scribbling in her new notebook. Hannah leaned over as far as she could, pretending to be interested. She hoped Bernice would look up at her and perhaps direct her to one of the empty places, but she seemed too engrossed in drawing large hearts with arrows through them and MOTHER written inside.

"Hey, watcha standin' for?" the boy named Billy shouted at her. "You the teacher or somethin'?"

"Nah, she's not a teacher," Arthur shouted back, but keeping his eyes on Hannah. "She's a you-know." He held his nose for a moment and snorted.

"Sit down, kid," Billy shouted again. He looked around and pointed to an empty desk. "There's a place."

Hannah smiled at him gratefully and slowly edged her way past pairs of legs stretched in the aisles to the empty desk. She sighed heavily and sat down.

The room was suddenly silent as Miss Hyatt entered. It was as if a lion tamer had walked into the room cracking his whip. But Miss Hyatt hardly looked like a lion tamer. She was a small woman with a wrinkled face, but her eyes, behind her glasses, were as black and shining as a bird's. Her hair was piled into a tight bun on top of her head; through the bun, a yellow pencil was thrust that seesawed up and down as she moved.

Billy grinned at the class as he was moved to the last seat in the last row and slumped down, his legs extending beyond the desk in front of him.

Hannah waited for the teacher to make some special announcement about her arrival and clutched and unclutched her fingers in anticipation. When the class found out that she had skipped a whole year and had been the smartest in her class and the one most often sent out to get old Mr. Benjamin's lunch, they would surely be sorry they had ignored her.

But Miss Hyatt merely nodded, not even looking straight at Hannah, and assigned her a seat with the same flat tone of voice as she had the others.

Hannah wondered if perhaps her old school had sent the wrong records. Maybe Miss Hyatt thought she was just an ordinary student. She raised her hand.

"Yes?" Miss Hyatt asked, and the class turned, at last, to look at her.

"I was just wondering," Hannah began, trying to keep her eyes on the teacher as twenty faces watched her with curiosity, "if you had all my records. I mean, for me, Hannah Brand."

"Yes, yes," Miss Hyatt said impatiently.

"Oh," Hannah said, not knowing what else to add. "Well, I was just wondering." She slid back into her seat and the other students turned back toward the teacher, disappointed that what Hannah had to say was not more interesting. It made her feel really foolish.

"Any more questions? Good, well now, eighth graders, I have something to say. You have now reached the beginning of the end, the first day of your final year at Spring Street School. You must set the example for the rest of the school, particularly as it involves your deportment in the halls as you go from class to class. All eyes will be upon you as you go, and it will bode little good should some innocent fourth grader glance up from his work to see a shuffling, noisy group of prospective eighth-grade graduates disrupting the decorum. Isn't that correct, William?" Miss Hyatt asked Billy.

"Huh?" Billy answered. "Oh, yeah, sure, Miss Hyatt."

The teacher cleared her throat, a signal that she was about to change the subject. "All right. Let us review."

"A new life?" Hannah thought. "The same old nouns and verbs and dangling participles." It would make no difference if she were a spy or a princess or anything else. They didn't even care that she was probably the youngest in the class. School was the same all over.

Eight

———◆◆———

AT LUNCHTIME, HANNAH LEANED AGAINST the rusted wrought-iron railing, clutching her lunchbox. She was very hungry, but waited to see if someone would invite her to sit with one of the groups that had gathered on the schoolyard steps. Ruth and Bernice were waving wildly at the twins, making what seemed to Hannah a great deal of noise trying to attract the attention of the two girls, who were not more than ten feet away. She supposed they were doing it to annoy her. They were succeeding.

She could smell the salami from Ruth's sandwich, and her stomach growled.

Cynthia, too, was making a fuss about surrounding herself with as many of her classmates as she could. "Lucille, here. I saved a place for you and Consuelo. Where's Edith? Tell Viola we're waiting," she called, keeping one eye on Hannah.

Hannah tried to remember who was who. Consuelo was the one Arthur had shoved off the seat, a tiny girl with very large brown eyes and a haircut so short it could barely contain the enormous pink bow that hung to one side. Viola, poor Viola, was perspiring in a heavy woolen sweater that hung loosely over a too-long skirt. Her straw-colored hair was plastered down over her forehead, and she kept jutting out her lower lip to blow it away. And Lucille was the prettiest girl Hannah had ever seen.

The steps were now crowded with girls, not only from her own class, but from several of the lower grades as well. There was much pushing and giggling as the boys tried to step over them in their rush to play ball before the period was over.

"Oh," Cynthia shrieked, "you horrible boy! Look what you did to my dessert." She held up a banana that looked as if it has been stepped on, which it had.

"It tastes better that way," Billy shouted back.

Hannah giggled, and Cynthia looked away from her squashed banana to glare at her.

Well, Hannah thought, at least she knows I'm here.

She sat down on the lowest step and opened her lunchbox. She wished she had brought a book with her so it would look as if she were so busy studying she had no time to talk to anyone. But she hadn't, so she munched her sandwich and watched the game of catch at the other end of the schoolyard.

"I spent the entire summer in the country," Cynthia was saying. "If it weren't for the mosquitoes, we would have had a wonderful time. Where did you go, Consuelo?"

"Are you kidding?" the tiny girl asked. "I spent the whole summer helping my father in the bakery. But, once, we took the day off and went to my aunt's in New Jersey."

"Poor darling," Cynthia said. "It must be terrible for you to have to work."

Hannah turned around and looked over her shoulder. She was hoping to see Consuelo push one of the custard pies from her father's bakery into Cynthia's face.

But Consuelo merely shrugged. "It's not so bad."

"How about you, Viola?" Cynthia asked sweetly. From the way she asked, Hannah guessed Cynthia must have some idea of the answer.

"Oh, I hung around. It was kind of nice, sleeping late in the morning." She sighed as if remembering the good old days.

"Well, I can imagine," Cynthia said. "Your mother must have kept you up all night."

There was sudden silence, and Hannah turned again, certain that they had all disappeared. No, they were still there. Viola was staring straight ahead, almost into Hannah's face, but she obviously didn't see her.

"Oh, I'm sorry. I shouldn't have brought that up, should I?" Cynthia said, not the least bit sorry at all.

"Why don't you ask Lucille about her summer?" Consuelo asked. "Tell her, Lucille."

"My father came up on weekends," Cynthia said quickly. "We all went out to dinner, to a different restaurant every Friday and Saturday night. I had to wear a dress." She looked around for sympathy at this announcement, but no one said anything. "I mean, in the summer, when it's hot, to wear a dress," Cynthia explained. "I mean, I was ever so much more comfortable in my shorts." She stretched her long legs straight out, almost kicking Hannah in the head.

"Hey," Hannah shouted. "Watch it with those big feet."

Consuelo giggled, and Lucille tried to hide her smile.

"But Lucille didn't tell you about her summer," Consuelo persisted. "She told me about it. How she went to"—she paused a moment to show that her next word would be very exciting—"Canada."

"Wow," Viola said. "That's really something. Did you take the train?"

44

"No, we drove," Lucille said. "We saw Quebec and Montreal."

"If I were going to Canada, I'd take the train. Driving is so tiring," Cynthia said, yawning. "Oh, was that the bell?"

But it was not quite time for the bell to ring. Lucille was asked about her journey. And Hannah, forgetting that she was not included in the group, turned around to listen. Even Ruth, Bernice, and the twins moved closer, and no one seemed to mind, except Cynthia.

"This is our conversation," she announced. "It's extremely rude to listen to other people's conversations. Or, maybe you didn't learn that in the Bronx," Cynthia said to Hannah. "Such manners."

"Oh, it's all right," Lucille said.

"Hah," Hannah snorted. "See?"

When the bell rang, Hannah rose with the others. She felt better, almost as if she had been invited to join in the discussion.

Nine

—••—

"HANNAH," MRS. BRAND CALLED. "YOUR friends are here."

"I don't have any friends," Hannah shouted back, but she came down the stairs quickly.

"Be nice, for a change," Mrs. Brand whispered as she held open the front door. "Come in, children."

"Hi," Ruth said. She stood in the doorway, glancing first toward Hannah and then at the group behind her. She motioned for them to come inside.

"What are you all dressed up for?" Hannah asked. Even Teddy looked as though someone had scrubbed his face, although his shirt was hanging out of his pants.

She was glad to see them but had decided not to be too friendly. After all, they had been in school for a whole week, and none of them had done more than just nod at her.

"We came from Sunday school," Teddy said. "I'm wearing my new shoes. See?" He held up one foot and lost his balance. "Pick me up, Bernice," he wailed to his sister.

Bernice moved forward and grabbed her brother by one arm. "You can get up by yourself," she mumbled. "I'm not your slave."

"So you came from Sunday school. Is that what you

wanted to tell me?" Hannah asked. "Make it snappy. We're having lunch."

"Well, it's connected," Ruth said. "We came because of something the rabbi told us there."

"Isn't that lovely," Mrs. Brand said. "That's lovely, children."

"How do you know it's so lovely, Ma?" Hannah asked. "They haven't said anything yet."

"If the rabbi said it, it must be—"

"Lovely," Hannah finished. "O.K., tell me already."

"Because Rosh Hashanah is coming," Reva began.

"On the Jewish New Year, we must forgive and forget," Carol finished.

"If anybody did anything mean to us during this past year—" Reva took up.

"—we have to forgive them and be friends," Carol said.

"And vice versa," Hannah added. "I know that stuff."

"So," Ruth said, "we decided that we would make up with you and start all over." She smiled at Hannah and gave Bernice's arm a tug. "Isn't that right?" she asked Bernice.

"M-m," Bernice grunted.

"I told you it would be lovely," Mrs. Brand said, although she wondered what Hannah had done to be forgiven. She patted Teddy on the head. "Take your time, children, but hurry up." She turned and went back to the kitchen.

"Does that mean you're forgiving me?" Hannah asked.

Ruth shook her head yes.

"But how about me forgiving you?" Hannah narrowed her eyes at Ruth and made a make-believe smile.

"What did we do?" Bernice asked. "Nothing!"

"Yeah? How would you like it if you didn't know anybody in town and you went to a strange school for a whole week and nobody ate lunch with you or told you where the bathroom was or the principal's name or anything? Hmm? How would you like that?" Hannah waited.

"It's the door next to the stairway and it has 'Girls' printed on it," Ruth's sister, Debbie, said quickly.

"And it's Miss Peterson," Carol said.

"The principal's name," Reva added.

"What else do you want to know?" Debbie asked eagerly.

"Be quiet," Ruth said to her sister. "Yeah, I suppose that wasn't nice," she said to Hannah. "We're sorry, aren't we?" She turned to the others who nodded.

"Will you be our friend now?" Reva asked.

"I'll have to think about it," Hannah said slowly.

"Please?" Carol pleaded.

"Pretty please?" Reva asked.

"I'll let you see my tooth that fell out," Teddy said.

"Butt out," Bernice said to her brother angrily.

"O.K.," Hannah said, after a moment, "I'll be your friend, but don't let it happen again."

"Ooh, thanks, Hannah," Debbie squealed, squeezing Hannah's hand.

"From now on, we're going to call for you every morning and we'll all walk to school together," Ruth said.

"Isn't that swell, Hannah?" Zack cried, jumping up and down in make-believe excitement. He moved forward and began to turn everyone toward the door. "So long, girls and boy." He gave Teddy a gentle push.

They stood on the porch waving, except for Bernice who was whispering to Ruth.

"Forget it," Ruth whispered back.

"But, we did and she didn't," Bernice was saying angrily. "We apologized and she didn't."

"Oh, come on," Ruth said and glanced back at Hannah who was smiling. "See you tomorrow," Ruth called.

"If you're lucky," Hannah called back.

Ten

———— ❖ ————

OF ALL THE STUDENTS IN THE EIGHTH grade, Lucille Travis was the one Hannah admired most. She wasn't the smartest, but she was the neatest and the prettiest. The collars of her blouses were perfect semicircles without a crease or curl. The cuffs on her socks were always neatly folded over and reached exactly the same height on each leg. Her brown hair waved carefully into the small gold barrette to one side and flipped at her shoulders into a soft curl. No matter how the wind blew, it seemed to veer around Lucille's head, leaving no sign of wisps or stray strands.

When Lucille answered a question in class, and she was called on only when she raised her hand, her voice was soft and clear. Her answers were always right, but she would end her sentences with a modest question mark as if she could be wrong and would be ever so grateful to be corrected.

Hannah listened, hypnotized by the rhythm of Lucille's words, and later, in front of the bathroom mirror, would try to imitate her. But, somehow, she always sounded like the grocer on the corner of Tremont Avenue, who had a habit of cheating his customers. "You think I put the rotten strawberries on the bottom?"

It seemed obvious to Hannah that Lucille liked her, too. She always waved when Hannah entered the schoolyard and would often laugh her tinkling, gentle laugh when Hannah said something funny. But it was not Lucille's perfection that, after a while, Hannah became used to, as everyone else in the class seemed to have done long ago—except Cynthia, who every morning gushed about Lucille's "stunning outfit." It was something else that made Hannah admire her, and it was not until she had heard Miss Hyatt, for the dozenth time, ask Lucille to fetch some papers from the principal's office, that she realized what it was.

"She's me," Hannah said to herself, with some surprise. "She's the favorite at Spring Street School that I used to be with Mr. Benjamin." Now that she had found the answer, Hannah could see other similarities. Didn't Lucille have a bunch of other kids following her around arguing about who would sit next to her at lunchtime? That was how it had been with her when Shirley and her other old friends ate lunch. Ah, she and Lucille had so much in common, no wonder they were becoming friends. Hannah decided to tell Lucille this, and she pictured how she and Lucille would giggle together about running all those errands for the lazy teachers and how hard it was to make a fair decision about who would get the honor of sharing the top step at lunch period.

Of course, Ruth would still be a close friend, too, Hannah thought, but Ruth was like another Shirley— comfortable, but not quite equal. That isn't nice, Hannah would tell herself. "I must learn to be kind to those less fortunate, the way Lucille is." And when she remembered, she would put her arm around Ruth's shoulders and smile at her, which might startle Ruth but would also please her.

"Mrs. Wells is back," Consuelo announced. "Get ready for trouble." She rolled her enormous brown eyes and pouted.

"How come she wasn't here the first two weeks?" Hannah asked.

"Sick, probably," Ruth said. "Mrs. Wells gets terrible headaches sometimes. That's why she's so mean."

"You won't have to worry, though, Hannah. You're smart," Lucille said.

"Gee thanks," Hannah muttered, feeling stupid for grinning so widely.

"She doesn't look so bad to me," Hannah wrote on a note and passed it over her shoulder to Ruth, as soon as they entered Mrs. Wells's classroom.

The teacher rose from her chair as if she had been glued to it. Slowly she gazed around the room. "Well, well," she said, "look who's back." She pointed to Billy Hermann, who was slumped in his seat, his long legs reaching well beyond the desk in front of his. "You're a sight for sore eyes," the teacher said.

Billy grinned. "You, too, Miz Wells."

"Stand up when I'm speaking to you, Billy," Mrs. Wells said softly and then suddenly shouted so loudly that the class jumped in their seats. "You big galoot! You give me any trouble this year, and you'll be out on your ear."

"Come on, Miz Wells. It's only the first day. I didn't do nuthin'," Billy said.

"And you better not," the teacher said, her voice returning to its softness. "Now, sit down."

He sat, sighing deeply, and Hannah felt sorry for him.

She waited to see if anyone else would be yelled at and followed the teacher's glance around the room. Hannah swallowed. Mrs. Wells was looking at her.

"And whom have we here?" she said.

Hannah pointed to herself. "Me?" she asked.

"Yes, you, my dear. Someone new to add sparkle and wit to this bunch of dummies?"

Hannah giggled.

"It's nice that you appreciate my little jokes. Now what is your name, or is that a secret?"

"Hannah Brand."

"Hannah Deanna Brand," Cynthia called from the back of the room.

"That will be enough, Cynthia," Mrs. Wells said.

Hannah wanted to turn around and stick her tongue out at Cynthia, but she was afraid to take her eyes off Mrs. Wells.

"Where are you from?" Mrs. Wells asked, tapping her pencil against her teeth, which were the same shade of faded yellow as her hair.

"The Bronx," Hannah answered. "I went—I attended—"

Mrs. Wells yawned without covering her mouth. It was a long yawn, and Hannah fidgeted as she stood. "We'll hear your life story some other time, Hannah Deanna. Sit down."

Hannah sighed deeply and sat down. Mrs. Wells was really funny, she thought.

"She sounds nuts to me," Zack said when Hannah told her family about her day at school that evening.

"She gets bad headaches, Ruth said," Hannah reported.

"Who's Ruth? Her doctor?" Zack asked.

"Ruth. Ruth Cohen, my friend, you know," Hannah said impatiently. "But Lucille said I don't have to worry because I'm smart. Those were Lucille's exact words." Hannah smiled as she remembered the moment.

"Who's Lucille? The principal?" Zack teased.

"Lucille is a girl in my class," Hannah said. "There are lots of good kids in my class. I really like them." She wanted to say more about Lucille, but was sure her brother would tease her. Instead, she told them about Viola who had to wear woolen sweaters even when the weather was warm because her mother didn't like to iron cotton blouses.

"*Goyim*," Mrs. Brand said. "What can you expect?"

"Hey, Ma, that's not a nice thing to say," Zack argued. "Just because a person isn't Jewish doesn't mean she's a bad mother."

"Did I say that?" Mrs. Brand asked. "I said no such thing."

"Maybe Viola's mother is sick—or old. Maybe they're too poor to have an iron," Hannah said angrily.

"Nobody's too poor to have an iron. Nobody should let a child go to school sweating and hot because she's lazy." Mrs. Brand waved a fork at Hannah.

"You know," Zack said, "I'll bet right this minute Viola's mother is telling her not to get too friendly with the new girl"—he pointed at Hannah and winked—"because you know what Jews are like, right?"

"What are we like?" Mrs. Brand asked slowly. "I'm interested."

"Oh, pushy and loud and Hannah will probably steal Viola's sweater and sell it on a pushcart. Jews are always out to get your money." Zack bent and squeezed his shoulders toward his head. He held out one hand and rubbed his thumb against his fingers.

"Even in a joke, it's not funny," Mrs. Brand said. "It's enough the *goyim* talk like that."

Zack straightened up. "See?" he asked, pointing a finger at his mother. "You don't like it when someone stereotypes the Jews. So, why should you make generalities about non-Jews, the *goyim,* as you so nicely put it?" He made a face as if he smelled something rotten.

"Yeah, Ma," Hannah said, although she was not quite sure she had understood everything her brother had said.

Mrs. Brand sighed and looked at her husband as if to ask how they had managed to raise such stupid children. Then she turned back to Zack, "Because, Mr. High School Sophomore who thinks his mother doesn't understand his big words, it's different. In Europe nobody is smashing the windows of Christian shopkeepers, nobody is throwing them out of schools and arresting them!"

Hannah yawned. She was sorry she had brought up the whole subject. What had started this, anyway, she wondered. Her father's next words reminded her.

"All this discussion because some poor child in Hannah's class wears a sweater on a warm day." He laughed. "Enough, already."

Eleven

———◆◆———

IT FELT FUNNY, AS IT ALWAYS HAD, STAYING
home from school in the middle of the week when you
weren't sick. As Hannah dressed, she looked out her
window and watched Cynthia get into her father's car
and be driven to school. Then Arthur, in a bright red
and white checked shirt, passed below, moving suddenly
into the street as he neared the Brands' house and walking in the middle of the road until he was well beyond.
Hannah saw him glance over his shoulder, and she drew
back quickly from the window.

When she came downstairs, her mother was setting
the dining-room table. Hannah giggled.

"You look funny doing that with your hat on," she
said. But her mother looked very nice. She was wearing
a new blue dress and had a string of beads around her
neck. The feather in her hat waved as she moved around
the table with the silverware.

"We just finished breakfast and you're setting the
table for lunch," Hannah said.

Her mother looked up at her. "I don't like to rush,
and when we come back from *shul*, everything will be
ready." She examined the table and sighed. "Ah, such a
few people," she said unhappily as she saw the four
place settings. "It will hardly seem like Rosh Hashanah

without everybody here. But your grandparents and Aunt Stella refused to ride on the Holy Days."

"Anyway," Hannah said, "it will be less work for you." But she agreed with her mother. What was a Jewish holiday without the whole family around?

"Work? To cook for your family? That's not work. It's a pleasure." She shook her finger at her daughter. "You'll remember these words when I'm gone."

"I'll write them in my book of Mrs. Brand's Wise Sayings," Hannah mumbled.

"So, let me look at you," Mrs. Brand said as her husband and son came down the stairs. "We have to make a good impression for this new *shul*. God forbid the members of the congregation should think I have *shlumps* in my family." She shook her head in approval, but couldn't resist brushing off her husband's lapel even though there was nothing to brush off.

"No *shlumps?* We're all neat and clean?" Mr. Brand asked his wife impatiently. "Then let's go. Zack, here's your tallis bag and here's mine." He picked up two small velvet bags which contained their prayer shawls and skullcaps and handed one to his son.

Slowly, they walked out the door and down the steps. Hannah felt stiff and shining in her new dress. It had a sailor collar and bright silver buttons down the front. Her hat was last year's, but it matched, and Hannah wished that Lucille could see her now, looking all neat and put together. She wondered if Cynthia would like her "outfit."

"Hey, there's Ruth," Hannah called out as they approached the synagogue. She tried to slip past her parents, but Mrs. Brand held her arm.

"You'll stay with us, please," her mother said.

Ruth's parents had stopped and turned, however, apparently waiting for the Brands to catch up. The two families crowded the sidewalk as everyone was introduced, while Mrs. Cohen apologized for not having welcomed the Brands to Hazelton with one of her famous chocolate cakes. But perhaps today, after dinner, if the Brands were going to be home . . .

"Where would we go?" Mrs. Brand asked. "It would make me very happy if you would be our guests for tea." She smiled happily at Mrs. Cohen, and Hannah saw her eyes grow bright as tears almost came.

"It's funny," she whispered to Zack. "I never thought about Ma being lonely and wanting friends, too."

The Hazelton Jewish Center was very much smaller than the old, onion-domed synagogue on Tremont Avenue. It was a square yellow-brick building with a wooden Star of David over the front door. The steps were crowded with congregants shaking hands and wishing each other a Happy New Year. Two men came over to Hannah's father and greeted him. "It's an honor to have such a scholar among us, Mr. Brand. Welcome."

Mr. Brand shook his head. "I'm far from a scholar, Mr. Rabinowitz. I have barely dipped my toe into the vast sea of Jewish writings."

Hannah almost laughed. Her father's words sounded like something from a book. At least, she thought, he never talked like that at home.

The service had already begun, had in fact been going on for more than an hour, but only the old men and boys who had just become bar mitzvahs, boys who were still enthusiastic about their prayers, attended from the beginning. Most people arrived in time for the Torah reading.

"Same stuff," Hannah whispered to Zack, as she

handed him a prayer book. "Just like in the Bronx." But it made her feel comfortable to sing the same melodies, read the same words as she had for the past holidays. She sang loudly, too, so that Ruth and whoever else was nearby would know she was at home in a synagogue and that she could read the Hebrew of the prayer book. Her father had taught her with surprising patience, and Hannah had learned to read and write Hebrew in spite of her boredom with the lessons.

Last summer, when she had gone to camp for two weeks, Mr. Brand had written to Hannah in Hebrew. She had sat on her cot, trying to puzzle out the sentences and eventually giving up. She thought it was mean of her father to expect her to understand the letters, and wrote back on postcards one of the few sentences she knew in Hebrew that would make sense: *Kawl ba seder.* "Everything is all right."

The month before, when she had helped her mother pack for the move to Hazelton, Hannah had found the two postcards in her father's summer jacket. The three words scratched into one corner of the cards, so that no one could tell what was written, looked stupid. She wondered why her father had saved them. Hannah had torn them into tiny pieces and flushed them down the toilet.

The edge of the wooden pew was hard and kept cutting into the back of Hannah's knees. She shifted and fidgeted and was always the first to rise when the Holy Ark was opened to reveal the Torahs. The scrolls, the Five Books of Moses, were wrapped in orange velvet and crowned with small silver pieces that jingled as they were carried around the room. To hold the Torahs, to open the Ark, to be called to the pulpit was an honor, and the greatest honor was to read the *maftir,* the portion of the week. Not many men could do it. It required special training.

"Ya'amod, maftir," sang the rabbi, and the congregation looked around to see who had been given this special honor.

Mr. Brand rose from his seat on the aisle and walked up the steps to the pulpit. There was buzzing throughout the room, and Hannah heard several people ask, "Who is he?"

He shook hands with the men around the lectern on which the Torah had been placed, kissed the fringes of his prayer shawl and touched them to the scroll and began. First a blessing and then, bending over to see the words more easily, he began.

The portion was, as it had always been on the first day of Rosh Hashanah in synagogues throughout the world, the story of an earlier Hannah, the Biblical Hannah, and of how, in return for God's granting her prayer for a son, she sent that child to serve in the Holy Temple. He became, of course, the great prophet Samuel.

Mr. Brand chanted, taking a breath now and then, but never hesitating. Mrs. Brand, sitting beside Hannah, kept clutching and unclutching her hands nervously, and when her husband had finished and looked up from the reading with a smile, she let out a deep, relieved sigh.

"Hey, why didn't Pa tell us he had *maftir?*" Zack whispered.

"He didn't tell me either," Mrs. Brand said. "He knows how nervous I get."

"Why? Didn't you know he was a scholar?" Hannah asked.

"I knew, I knew, but who knew?" Mrs. Brand answered, and Hannah giggled.

Twelve

———•◆•———

"THAT WAS A *YOM TOV* MEAL?" MR. BRAND
asked as his wife slid his coffee cup from under his hands.
"You didn't give me a chance to finish anything." He
looked annoyed for a moment, then he smiled. "I
haven't seen you look so happy since we moved here,
Lillie. I think you invited the whole *shul* for this afternoon."

"It will be a real *Yom Tov*, a holiday," Mrs. Brand
said. "It's been a long time since we had people
here."

"What are we?" Zack asked. "Laughing hyenas?"

"Hannah, go fluff up the sofa cushions and see that
the living room is neat." Mrs. Brand rushed from the
dining room to the kitchen, cleaning up the holiday
plates and giving orders to her husband and children.
"Make sure the bathroom is straightened out. Zack,
reach up to the top shelf and get me the silver tray for
the cake."

"Not so fast, Ma," Hannah said. "I forgot what the
first thing you told me to do was." She stood in the
middle of the living room, trying to remember.

"The cushions, the cushions," Mrs. Brand called from
the kitchen.

Hannah patted the sofa. "What good will it do? The
minute someone sits down it will be flat again," she
yelled.

"Never mind. Do what your mother asked," Mr. Brand said. "Lillie, where are my cigars?"

"That's important at this moment? To smell up the house with your cigars? Go out on the porch and smoke." She had finished in the kitchen and now went from room to room, examining each as she thought a stranger might. "Zack, your room," she called. "Pick up your books. I'll be embarrassed if someone sees." She walked over to Hannah, brushed down her hair with her hand and turned her around slowly.

"Are you going to sell her to the highest bidder?" Zack asked.

"Ma, they already saw me at services. Cut it out," Hannah said.

Mrs. Brand sighed. There seemed to be nothing more to do, so she sat on the edge of the piano bench and waited. When the doorbell rang, she jumped up. "The coffee. I forgot the coffee. Get the bell, somebody."

Within several minutes, the house was filled with guests, many of whom the Brands had met only that morning at the synagogue. Each time someone had come over to congratulate Mr. Brand on his Torah reading, Mrs. Brand had invited them for coffee and cake that afternoon. It seemed to Hannah that nobody refused.

"You certainly have a fine-looking family," Mr. Rabinowitz told Hannah's father. He pinched Hannah's cheek and then patted it. "The Ackermanns have a daughter about your age, young lady."

Hannah looked around. "Which ones are the Ackermanns?"

"Oh, not yet. They're not here yet, but they're coming soon, God willing."

"I'll save some cake," Hannah said.

Mr. Rabinowitz laughed. "Not that soon. There's still a lot to do before they come."

Hannah nodded her head, although she had no idea what he was talking about.

"I heard Mr. Rabinowitz mention the Ackermanns," Ruth said, stuffing some cookies into her mouth. "Isn't it exciting?"

She pulled the tray away from Ruth's hands. "Who are they?"

"The refugees," Ruth said. "Didn't you know? A doctor and his family from Germany. We're helping them escape from Hitler."

"What did you do?" Hannah asked. "Build an underground tunnel?"

"Raised money," Ruth said. "And wrote letters to President Roosevelt. It costs a lot of money to get a family out of Germany."

"When will they get here?" Hannah asked.

"Nobody knows. Hitler keeps changing his mind and asking for more money and stuff."

"He's mean," Debbie said, coming over to look for something to eat. "He kills people and smashes their stores and everything. Can I have a drink of water?"

"Debbie, we're talking about something serious. Go away," Ruth said. "It does seem strange, though, us here having a good time and over there"—she waved her arm in the direction she thought Europe would be—"people being killed and hiding in attics and everything." She bent over to straighten the seams in her stockings. "My mother lent me these. It's the first time."

"Listen," Hannah said, "let's go out on the porch. It's hot in here and I don't know anybody." She pulled Ruth toward the front door, but Ruth hung back. "What's the matter?"

"I don't feel like going outside," Ruth said. "You know, all the kids are home from school now, and I feel funny all dressed up like this."

Hannah shrugged. "O.K., do what you want. I'm going." She brushed past several people and finally reached the porch. She wasn't alone. Several men were sitting in the old rockers, talking. They looked up when Hannah appeared.

"Come, young lady, sit down," an elderly man said as he rose from his chair.

"No, thanks. I have to get something down the street for a minute," Hannah lied. "My mother may need another tray."

The men would ask her her name, say she was a smart girl, and then go on discussing what they had before. She would be forced to sit in the rocker like a prisoner and pretend to be interested. She ran down the steps quickly, as if she really had something important to do.

But there was nothing to do, nowhere to go. Slowly, Hannah walked up the street, looking back over her shoulder to see if the men were watching her. They were.

Cynthia was sitting on her front stoop throwing a ball in the air. "Can you come over?" she called.

"I can, but I'm not sure I want to," Hannah yelled back.

"I want to tell you something," Cynthia shouted.

Hannah walked across the street, careful not to dirty her black patent-leather pumps. She wished she was wearing stockings like Ruth's so that her legs would look longer. "Speak or forever hold your peace," she said as she approached Cynthia.

Cynthia looked at Hannah carefully. "Boy, you sure are dressed up."

"It's my new outfit," Hannah said, hoping Cynthia would hear her sarcasm.

"What's going on? A party or something?" Cynthia asked, pointing her chin toward Hannah's house.

"That's for me to know and you to find out," Hannah said. "As it happens, my parents have invited a few friends over for tea."

"In the middle of the week? How come?"

"It's a holiday. A Holy Day. You wouldn't know about such things."

"Sure I would," Cynthia said. "It's the Jewish New Year."

Hannah's eyes widened in surprise. "Gee, you're not as dumb as you look," she mumbled.

"You'd be surprised at what I know," Cynthia said mysteriously.

"If it's more than one and one makes two, I would be," Hannah sneered. "What did you want to tell me. I'm busy." She looked around to see if anyone was watching her. She was not quite sure whether she should be talking to Cynthia on a Jewish holiday. Perhaps there was some kind of rule that made it less holy if you spoke to someone who wasn't Jewish. Well, anyway, nobody had ever told her about it.

"Consuelo asked if you were sick or something," Cynthia said.

"What did you tell her?" Hannah asked.

"The truth." Cynthia smiled, inviting Hannah to ask more questions.

Hannah shrugged, and Cynthia looked disappointed. She shaded her eyes and peered at Hannah's house.

"You know a lot of people for somebody who practically just moved here," she said.

"Oh, we get around," Hannah said. "Listen, what did you want to tell me?"

Cynthia closed her eyes and tried to look mysterious. "Lucille is having a party."

"Really?" Hannah asked. "Is it her birthday or something?" She tried to remember where she had put the Hanukkah money her grandfather had given her last winter. She would have to buy a present.

"People don't have to have birthdays to give a party," Cynthia sneered. "People like Lucille can have them just for no reason at all."

"Are you invited?" Hannah asked, although she didn't want to.

"Of course. How else would I know about it?" She folded her arms and waited for Hannah's next question.

"I know about it, too," Hannah said.

Cynthia jumped down from where she was sitting. "You know about it? How?"

"You just told me, dummy," Hannah said. "Ha, ha."

"Oh." Cynthia sighed, relieved. "I thought . . ."

"Well, of course I wasn't in school today, so Lucille didn't have a chance to invite me," Hannah said. She was sure that was the reason. Lucille liked her. She was sure of that, too. Hadn't she told Hannah she was smart?

"Well, don't count on it. Lucille wasn't sure until you were absent today," Cynthia advised. "I mean, don't expect to be invited."

"Why not?" Hannah asked, genuinely surprised.

"Ruth and Bernice weren't invited, either. Does that answer your question?" Cynthia said.

Hannah was confused. "Was Consuelo?"

"Of course!"

"And Viola?"

"Certainly. And Arthur and Walter Sorg and—I don't remember who else."

"Billy Hermann?"

Cynthia burst out laughing. Not real laughter, but it made her cough.

Hannah took the opportunity to pound her on the

66

back. "Does this help?" she asked, giving Cynthia a solid whack.

"Hey, that hurts. Quit it," Cynthia shouted. "Of course not Billy Hermann. Lucille doesn't want any big galoots at her party."

"Ruth and Bernice aren't galoots. Well, Ruth isn't, anyway," Hannah said.

"That's all I'm going to tell you," Cynthia said. She walked toward her doorway and stood there. "But think about it, Hannah, and don't count on Lucille being your friend." She twirled around, almost tripping on the small doorstep, and closed the door behind her.

"I'm thinking," Hannah mumbled to herself. "But! I don't believe you, Cynthia Shmynthia." And she turned back to her house in time to see her mother waving at her to come home.

Thirteen

"WHAT DO YOU MEAN, I MISSED A BIG TEST?" Hannah asked Cynthia when she saw her in the school-yard.

"Mrs. Wells gave us an arithmetic test that will count for half of our first report card," Cynthia repeated.

"She always does that," Ruth said. "I heard about it."

"Well, what about us?" Hannah asked, getting angrier by the second. "We were absent."

"That's your problem," Cynthia said over her shoulder as she walked away.

"Let's ask if we can make it up," Hannah said to Ruth. "She sometimes lets Bernice make up tests when she's out sick."

Ruth held up her hands. "Not me. I'm not asking her anything."

She sat in Miss Hyatt's class, thinking about whether to talk to Mrs. Wells, and was surprised when she saw everyone shuffle out of the room. She hadn't heard a word of what had been going on and glanced at the blackboard to see what the lesson had been.

As they entered the arithmetic class, Ruth nudged Hannah. "Are you going to?" she whispered.

"You bet!" Hannah said, but when she looked at Mrs. Wells standing by her desk with her arms folded, Hannah wondered if she dared.

Ruth had apparently told Bernice what Hannah had said, and the two girls stared at Hannah, waiting.

"Don't worry, I will," Hannah whispered and raised her hand.

At first, Mrs. Wells ignored her as she usually did, but Hannah kept her hand raised although it had begun to ache.

"What is it?" Mrs. Wells said at last.

Hannah took a deep breath. "I heard . . ." She looked at Ruth. "I mean, *we* heard that you gave a test when we were absent, and we were wondering if we could please make it up after school."

Ruth had her head down and was trying to make herself as small as possible in her seat. She looked neither at Hannah nor at the teacher.

"You mean that you expect me to take my own time after school and hang around here while you take a test?"

Hannah nodded.

"Look, young lady, if you can't do your work during regular school hours, that's just too bad. Now sit down." She picked up a book and began turning pages.

"But, it was a Jewish holiday. We had to be absent," Hannah said.

Mrs. Wells looked quickly at Hannah and slammed the book down on the desk. "It may interest you to know that this is an American school. We don't observe every mumbo-jumbo holiday that you people stay home for."

"We didn't stay home. We went to synagogue," Hannah explained. Did Mrs. Wells think that they just hung around and listened to the radio or played ball or something?

"I have just about had enough of this. I'm not the least bit interested," Mrs. Wells shouted.

The class began to giggle nervously as her voice rose. "You mean we can't make up the test? I don't think that's fair," Hannah shouted back. She watched, almost hypnotized, as Mrs. Wells moved toward her, and was startled to find the teacher's fingers on her arm, growing tighter and tighter.

There was a sudden pull, and Hannah found herself tripping down the aisle. She held out her arms to keep from falling.

"I see London, I see France, I see Hannah's underpants," Arthur sang softly, and when Hannah looked up at him, he stuck out his tongue.

Hannah stood where she had almost fallen and wondered whether she was supposed to go back to her seat or what? But Mrs. Wells was blocking her way. They stared at each other, Hannah determined not to lower her eyes until the teacher had. Finally, Mrs. Wells looked at her watch. "You've wasted enough of my time. Now get back to your seat and behave yourself. You're a troublemaker, I can see that."

Hannah lowered her head and smiled. At least Ruth would know that when Hannah said she'd do something, she'd do it. But as she sat there, she knew that Mrs. Wells had really won. She could give Hannah a *D* on her report card, a mark Hannah had never received in her life.

"I don't think you should have done that," Ruth told her as they walked home.

"I was only standing up for my rights," Hannah said. "She has a lot of nerve." She rubbed her arm where the teacher's fingers had dug in.

"Yeah, but Hannah, we're not supposed to do those things," Ruth said softly. "It only makes things worse."

There were sudden footsteps behind them, and before they could run, Hannah felt a sharp whack on her back.

"Hey," she shouted, almost stumbling.

"Kid, I got to hand it to you. You got guts," a deep voice said.

Hannah looked up into Billy Hermann's face. He was grinning at her, and Hannah guessed that the whack was meant to be friendly.

"Boy, you don't have to knock me down," Hannah said.

Billy seemed as if he was about to cry. "Oh, gee, I'm sorry. Did I hurt you, kid?" He moved to brush off her skirt, but she stopped his hand.

"I'm all right."

"Well, anyway," Billy said happily, "I think you did swell. If I was you, though, I would have given the old bag a punch in the nose." He made a fist and swung at the air. Hannah ducked. "Listen, if you ever want me to give her a punch in the nose, just say the word," he said, patting Hannah on the shoulder. "You're really a tough kid." He waved and walked away. "Hey, Hannah," he called over his shoulder. "Not only the old bag. I mean anybody who bothers you." He made another swing of his fist in the air and disappeared around a corner.

Hannah and Ruth stared after him.

"My hero." Hannah giggled, clutching her chest and rolling her eyes. But even while she was making fun of Billy, she felt a little guilty. After all, he was trying to be friendly.

"Yeah, two of a kind," Ruth said without smiling. "You and Billy."

"What does that mean? I'm not dopey."

"Not much!" Ruth said. "You sure got us into trouble today." She walked away from Hannah quickly.

"Hey, what are you mad about?" Hannah called after her. "All I did was stand up for our rights."

Ruth whirled around. "Not my rights. Keep me out of this."

Hannah was startled. Ruth was usually so sweet, but now she was angry and facing Hannah with tight lips and narrowed eyes. "You just better not make any more trouble for the rest of us," she said. "It's bad enough as it is."

Fourteen

"HANNAH," ZACK CALLED, "YOUR BOY-friend's here again."

"Tell him to get lost. I don't want to see him. And he's not my boyfriend," Hannah yelled back. She pushed her sweaters into her dresser drawer and stood examining her face in the mirror. Billy Hermann had told her she was pretty, which had made Ruth shriek with laughter and which Hannah didn't believe for a minute. Her eyeglasses made her look like an owl, and her hair seemed never to go in the right directions. She licked her finger and tried to smooth down the top of her head, but the hair kept jumping up as if it were on springs.

"He's been here every afternoon for the past week," she said as she came down the stairs. "What a pest!"

"Hiya, Hannah, your brother and his friend let me in," Billy said as if he hadn't heard what Hannah had called him. "What's your name, again?" he asked Irwin, who was watching Billy with a wide smile on his face.

"Michael Mouse, but my friends call me Mickey," Irwin said.

"No kiddin'?" Billy asked. "You know there's a movie actor by that name."

"No kiddin'?" Irwin mimicked and looked surprised

as if this was the first time he had heard about it. "I may have to sue."

"Billy, what are you doing here again?" Hannah asked. "Don't you have any friends?"

"That's not a nice thing to say, Hannah," Zack said, shaking a finger at his sister. "Where are your manners? Ask the gentleman to sit down. Offer him some tea and cookies." He poked Irwin in the ribs and winked.

"Nah, that's O.K. I ain't hungry. I just came over to see Hannah here. I thought maybe she'd like to go for a soda down at the drugstore."

"Well now, that's an exciting proposition, isn't it Ir . . . I mean, Mickey, old man?" Zack asked.

Billy smiled at him gratefully. "You guys can come, too," he said. "I got plenty of dough."

"Oh, we wouldn't dream of intruding on your tête-à-tête," Irwin said, shaking his head violently. "That's French for"—he rolled his round eyes at Zack—"romance."

Hannah watched Zack and Irwin, trying hard not to laugh. If she did, then Billy would realize they were teasing him and might get angry. He was as big as Zack and almost twice as tall as Irwin.

"I can't go, Billy. My mother says I have to help her," Hannah said.

"Do what?" Billy asked. "I'll help, too, and then we can get it done faster and then you can come." He started to remove his jacket.

"No," Hannah said quickly. "It's something you don't know how to do."

"What?" Billy asked, scratching his head.

"Yes, what, Hannah?" Zack asked. He folded his arms and waited.

74

Hannah made a face at her brother. "Shorten some dresses."

"Oh," Billy said, disappointed. "I don't think I can do that, Hannah."

"No, no, it's all right," Zack said, handing Billy back his jacket. "Irwin and I will help my mother. Irwin is wonderful with a needle and thread."

"Honest?" Billy asked. "I never heard of no guys sewing." He looked at Irwin's pudgy hands with amazement.

"Neither did I," Hannah said. "He's only fooling."

"Just for a little while," Billy pleaded. "It don't take long to drink a soda."

"Billy, I'm only twelve years old," Hannah said. "My parents say I'm not allowed to go out with boys." This was not true, Hannah knew, but only because the subject had never come up.

"Oh, I ain't a boy," Billy said stupidly.

"Right, he's a gorilla," Zack muttered to Irwin, and then as if he suddenly realized that his sister shouldn't go out with Billy, he turned to him. "Hannah's right, Bill, old man, my mother won't let her."

Hannah sighed.

"But, Jeez, I have this money." He jingled some coins in his pocket.

"Sounds like a lot," Irwin said.

"It is. I work sometimes after school loadin' boxes down by the railroad." He smiled proudly, and Zack and Irwin tried to look impressed. "But, if Hannah won't go with me, I won't have nothin' to do this afternoon. Hey, wait a minute," he said, slapping his palm hard against his forehead. "I just thought of somethin'. I have this note here. . . ." He patted his jacket and then pulled out a small piece of paper from his trouser pocket. "Cynthia give it to me." He handed the note to Hannah.

"Lucille is having a party on the second at seven o'clock and wants you to come. Tell Hannah that she's invited, too," Hannah read.

"I could walk over with you," Billy suggested. "It wouldn't be as if you was goin' with me. I could just keep you company on the way." He looked at Zack and Irwin hopefully. "Do you think your folks would say O.K.?"

"Well . . ." Zack began, looking quickly at Hannah for a clue about whether or not she wanted to go. "Friday night. It's the Sabbath."

"Cynthia gave you that?" Hannah asked. "It's a phony. Don't believe it."

Billy seemed confused. He scratched his head and took the note back from Hannah, examining the paper on both sides as if for secret writing, then reading each word over again very slowly. "Gosh, it says it clear as day," he announced. "Me and Hannah's invited to Lucille's party."

"But we're not, Billy. Cynthia told me we weren't invited. Clear as day," she emphasized. "Why didn't Lucille ask us herself, then?"

"Oh," Billy said, hopping up and down on one foot in excitement. "Cynthia explained that. She told me"— he gazed up at the ceiling trying to remember the exact words—"that she was helpin' Lucille with the invitations and that she lost this one and then she found it again, but she don't want Lucille to know that she give it to me so late, so I ain't supposed to say nothin' to Lucille." He nodded his head happily, satisfied with his memory.

"That sounds reasonable," Irwin said. "What do you think, Zachary, old man?"

Zack raised his eyebrows and pursed his lips. "I don't know. If you knew Cynthia—"

"—like I know Cynthia. Oh, oh, oh, what a girl," Irwin sang.

Billy stared at the two boys, bewildered. "Hey, these guys are really funny," he said, smiling at Hannah.

"Quiet!" Hannah shouted. "This is serious." She grabbed the note back from Billy. She really did want to go to Lucille's party. And so what if the invitation wasn't real? If they went to the party and showed Lucille the note, Lucille would surely let them in. She wasn't mean. She told Zack and Irwin what she was thinking.

"If she's not mean, how come she didn't ask you herself to begin with?" Zack suggested. "I don't think you should go. If they don't want you, keep away."

"But I want to go," Hannah whined.

"I wouldn't let nobody hurt Hannah," Billy said. "Let anybody just try." He made a fist and punched the air hard.

Zack ducked. "Boy, you have a mean right hook," he said. "But, if you're asking me about the party, I think you should forget it."

"You think?" Hannah shrieked. "Who are you? My father? You're only my brother. You have no right."

Zack shrugged. "Have it your own way. Come on, Irwin. Let's go down and shoot some baskets. It's getting late."

Irwin nodded. "You coming, Bill?" he asked.

"Sure," Billy said. He turned to Hannah. "Well, so long. I'll see you in school . . . if Miz Wells don't kick me out." He grinned at her, certain that she would appreciate this joke.

Hannah put her fingers to the sides of her mouth and stretched a smile. "Yeah," she said.

"Hey what's this on your door? This little metal thing?" Billy asked Zack as they left.

"A *mezuzah*," Zack said.

"A what?" Billy asked.

"A *mezuzah*," Zack repeated. "It's got some Hebrew words on it. You put it on the doorways of houses where Jewish people live."

"You Jewish?" Billy asked. "I didn't know that."

"Why? Does it make a difference?" Zack's jaw tightened.

"Why should it?" Billy asked, puzzled at the change in Zack's tone of voice. "I knew a guy once had a shrunken head for a door knocker. It's a free country."

Fifteen

HANNAH HAD NEVER SEEN HER BROTHER
look so unhappy. She had rarely seen him look unhappy
at all. But tonight, as they sat around the dinner table,
Hannah was the smiling one.

"Consuelo said that we have to buy material for our
graduation dresses soon," Hannah announced. "Consuelo said that the best place to get it is the Merrick
Fabric Shop. Consuelo said—"

" 'Consuelo said,' " Zachary said angrily. "Is that all
you can talk about? 'Consuelo said, Consuelo said,' " he
mimicked in a singsong tone.

Mr. Brand looked up from his plate. "Zachary, what's
wrong? You don't sound like yourself. Something wrong
at school?"

Zachary didn't answer. He sat there pushing his
mashed potatoes around with his fork.

"Your father asked you a question, Zachary," Mrs.
Brand reminded him. "Well, is there something wrong
at school?"

"I didn't make it," he mumbled.

"The team? Maybe they don't use sophomores," Mrs.
Brand suggested.

"Oh, they use sophomores. They even use freshmen.
They even use guys two inches shorter than me—"

Mr. Brand opened his mouth to correct him. "Than

I," he was about to say, but the words never came out.

"They even use guys on the scrub team who wouldn't know a layup from a jump shot," he continued. "At tryouts, do you know what I shot? Do you?" he asked his parents angrily.

They waited.

"Four out of five, do you believe it?"

Hannah and her parents shook their heads yes. "Oh, I believe it, Zack," Hannah said, trying to help. "Remember at camp how you used to—"

"Yeah, that's right." He shook his head.

"Maybe they want to use the people from last year," Mr. Brand said as if he didn't really think that at all.

"I'll tell you who they want to use and it's not me. You know why?"

Suddenly, Mr. and Mrs. Brand understood. They knew why.

"Why?" Hannah asked quickly, afraid the question would never be answered. "Why?"

"I can't believe it," Mr. Brand said. "Not in a public high school."

"Why?" Hannah whined.

"Oh, you'd better believe it," Zachary said. "It's happening all over the world."

"What is? What is?" Hannah shrieked. If someone didn't explain soon, she would blow up.

"Oh, Hannah, how could you be so dumb?" Zack muttered through his teeth.

Hannah was all mixed up. This was not her brother. He never talked to her that way. Oh, he teased her a lot, but he never said anything in that mean voice. And another thing, his eyes under their long lashes were filling with tears. "No, Zack," Hannah wanted to shout, "you never cry. What happened?" But she didn't. She just sat across from him aching to jump up and hug him, but she knew he would pull her arms from his shoulders, maybe even push her away.

"Who told you?" Mr. Brand asked. "I mean, did they say so in so many words?"

"Oh come on, Dad, you know that's not the way they do it. They posted a list on the bulletin board. My name wasn't on it. I went to see the coach to ask him if there was a mistake, or maybe if there was a scrub team they hadn't listed yet, or what?"

"What did he say?"

"He wasn't there. 'Coach Wiznowski is at a meeting,' one of the guys in the office told me, one of the guys on the team. They always hang around the office. They never seem to be in class."

"It's possible," Mrs. Brand said. "It's possible, Zack." She reached out her hand to pat her son's arm, but he pulled away.

"When I can see him, right there through the open door? And I can hear him laughing with some guys? Some meeting!"

"Did you say that?" Hannah asked. "I mean, did you tell somebody you knew he was there?"

"*He* knew I was there, and he knew I knew he was there. As a matter of fact, he looked straight at me when he leaned over to shut the door." Zack's face turned a deep red at the thought of his earlier embarrassment.

"But you haven't had an answer from him. I mean, you don't know definitely," Mr. Brand said. He turned his palms upward as if to explain that Zack's logic was at fault.

"Well, let me put it this way," Zack said. "Would you get the point if you heard someone say from behind that closed door, oh, just loud enough for me to hear, 'We don't need no Jewboys on *our* team.' " Zack sat back in his chair, finally calm, and began cutting his meat.

For a while, the only sound in the room was the scrape of Zack's knife against his plate. Then his father said softly, "It was a mistake."

Zack looked up. "It was no mistake."

"No, not what you told us. Moving here. It was a mistake. I should not have let my children be subjected to what I went through, what my father went through. In his day . . ." He stared out the dining-room window as if watching a play being acted somewhere beyond the rose bushes he had planted.

"What happened in your father's day?" Hannah asked. She wondered which twenty-four hours in her life would be called "Hannah's day."

"Don't ask," Mrs. Brand said. "It's better you don't know such things."

"Why not? It's part of their history," Mr. Brand said, returning his glance to his family. "Of course, I was only a small boy, maybe five or six, but I remember it clearly. I can see the Cossacks, the Russian soldiers of the Czar, stamping into our house and pulling my father from his bed. They wanted something from him. Maybe information about our neighbors. Maybe a glass of vodka. They always wanted something. Whatever it was, my father didn't have it."

"What did they do?" Zack asked, distracted for the moment from his unhappiness.

"What they always did," Mr. Brand said. "They beat him. I watched from beneath my bed until someone pulled me away. Somehow, I was pushed into a tunnel outside our house and then I found myself in a wagon,

82

covered by hay. I can still remember the sweetness of the odor, although it was very cold. I must have lain there for many hours. The next thing I remember, I was on a ship, a small boy all alone, traveling to the Golden Land, America." He sighed. "I never saw my father again, I never even knew he had died following his beating. I don't even know where he is buried."

"That's terrible," Hannah said, although she didn't feel the least bit sad. It was as if her father had been talking about strangers.

"I suppose you're telling me that, compared to what you went through, not making the high school basketball team is nothing," Zack said angrily.

Mr. Brand smiled at his son. "You're expecting an argument from me? You won't get it. I think what happened to you today is very serious. I only wish I knew how to help you."

"That's easy," Hannah said. "Let's converse."

"We are conversing," Zack told her. "We're talking to each other, and that's conversing."

Hannah bit her lip and thought for a moment. "Then that's not the word. I mean converse from our religion."

Zack laughed loudly, and although Hannah was annoyed that he was laughing at her, she was glad to see him amused. "You mean *convert,* dumbbell."

"What made you think of that, Hannah?" Mr. Brand asked slowly.

"I don't know," she said, not telling the truth. "It just seems that it's so much trouble being Jewish." As a matter of fact, she had been thinking about it since she had heard about Lucille's party. She had tried to figure out what she, Ruth, and Bernice had in common that would make them unwelcome. Billy didn't count.

She knew everybody thought he was just plain big and dumb. They were Jewish, the three of them, that's what it was. Lucille didn't want Jews at her party. At first, Hannah had refused to believe it. She was sure that Arthur had something to do with it. Lucille was too nice, and she talked to Hannah in school and had once told her that she had heard Miss Hyatt tell Miss Peterson, the principal, that Hannah had a good mind. She wouldn't do that if she didn't like her, Hannah was certain. But it was the only answer.

"It's a betrayal," Mrs. Brand was saying. "People who convert from Judaism are cowards and ignoramuses who don't know what they are giving up."

"Sure they do." Zack smirked. "A beating. Is that so hard to give up?"

"What's the matter with you, Zachary? Did you forget everything you ever learned?" Mr. Brand asked, his voice rising in anger. "Did you forget the story about the Martyrs, brave men like Rabbi Akiba, who had their eyes put out and their skin torn off rather than submit to barbarians who wanted them to—"

"Converse?" Zack interrupted, winking at Hannah.

But his father ignored his joke. "Or what happened at Masada where an entire community committed suicide rather than submit to the Romans? Or the Spanish Inquisition in 1492 when Jews were burned at the stake rather than submit to the church?"

"Oh, Pa, that's ancient history," Zack said. "It happened centuries ago."

"Never mind," his father replied. "Brave men are brave men whenever they lived."

"Then, I guess I'm a coward," Zack said with a sudden smile. "If I had the choice of being burned at the stake or playing on the basketball team, guess which one

84

I'd choose." He bent over and kissed the top of his father's head. "Don't worry, **Pa.** Only kidding. I'll stick with the God of Abraham, Isaac, and Jacob."

"Don't be blasphemous," Mrs. Brand said. But she smiled back at her son.

Sixteen

THERE WAS NO POINT BEATING ABOUT THE bush, Hannah decided. She would come right out and ask—and not Cynthia, who was a sneaky liar, but Lucille herself.

She had prepared for it all morning, first deciding to wear her prettiest outfit, as that rat, Cynthia, would call it, and her new shoes that she had gotten for the High Holidays. She wanted to look as much like Lucille as possible. While she stood before her dresser mirror, combing her hair, she practiced the words in a low whisper.

"Lucille, how come you didn't invite me to your party?"

She tried the question out several times, each time emphasizing a different word. "How come *you* . . . ?" "How come you *didn't* . . . ?" "How come you didn't invite *me* . . . ?" Hannah sighed. Well, it would work out at the time.

As she laid her comb back on the dresser scarf, she read Shirley's embroidered words. Hannah smiled. There had never been a party given by someone in her class that she and Shirley had not been invited to. And, boy, they were swell parties with lots to eat and good games like Hide and Seek and Pin the Tail on the Donkey. Well, actually, they were sort of baby parties, Hannah decided. Lucille's would, no doubt, be different. In what way, Hannah could not think. Perhaps they played records and danced. Zack had gone to a few of those and reported that they were boring. She wondered if Zack could dance. She couldn't, except for a silly imitation of Ginger Rogers whirling around the room. She wished, for the first time, that she was older—as old as Lucille and most of the others in her class who were already fourteen. Billy, she had heard, was fifteen. Hannah had always been proud of being the youngest in the class. It meant she had skipped and was obviously smarter than everyone else. Perhaps Lucille thought she was too young for her party. Maybe, if she borrowed her mother's lipstick . . .

"What are you doing up there, Hannah?" her mother called. "You'll be late. Ruth and Bernice are just passing the house."

Hannah flew down the stairs and gobbled her breakfast. "See ya, Ma," she said, grabbing her schoolbag and lunchbox.

"Wait, your lip is bleeding," her mother called after her. "Let me see."

But Hannah had slammed the door behind her and stood on the porch wiping off the lipstick on her sweater sleeve. Lucky the sweater was also red, Hannah thought as she examined it. The streaks were almost invisible.

"Ooh," Bernice said, drawing back, a look of disgust on her face. "What happened?"

"With what?" Hannah asked.

"Your mouth. It's all red," Bernice shrieked. "Wait, don't come near me. It might be catching."

"Let's see, let's see," Ruth begged. "It's bleeding gums, that's what it is. I knew a girl who had that once, and every time she sucked on an orange, all the blood—"

"Stop!" Bernice said. "I don't want to hear about it."

"Oh, it's nothing," Hannah said, disgusted at the fuss. "I wanted to see how I looked in lipstick. I thought I wiped it all off." She looked at her sleeve and shrugged. "Tell me where it is, and I'll wash it off with spit."

"Where it is?" Bernice asked. "It's all over your chin, that's where it is."

Hannah spit on her palm and rubbed her face. "Is that better?"

"No, it's still there. You better go back home and wash it off with soap and water," Ruth suggested.

"I can't. I'll be late, and there's something important I have to discuss with Lucille."

"What?" Ruth asked.

Hannah thought for a moment. She wondered if she should mention the party to the two girls who also weren't invited. Perhaps it wouldn't hurt to have their advice.

"You're not!" Ruth said, when Hannah told them the story. "Oh, you mustn't."

"Why?" Hannah asked. "I want to hear it from Lucille's own lips. I think maybe she told Cynthia to invite me and Cynthia didn't want—"

Ruth and Bernice were both shaking their heads violently. "No, no. We're not invited and that's that," they insisted.

"Don't ask for it, Hannah, and don't include us if you do," Ruth added. "Anyway, right now you look so awful, you'd better go to the bathroom and clean your face. Lucille would die laughing if she saw you."

Hannah covered her face with her hand and pretended she had a coughing fit as they entered the schoolyard. Quickly, she ran into the building, past one of the boys in her class who was the school door monitor and who shouted, "Hey, Hannah, nobody's allowed in yet. The bell didn't ring."

"Chuch, chuch," Hannah coughed, keeping one hand over her mouth. With the other, she pointed to the door marked "Girls," and the boy drew back, embarrassed. "O.K., but hurry up," he said.

With a soiled hand towel that had been shared by whoever used the lavatory for the past few days, Hannah scrubbed her face. When she thought she had cleaned off the lipstick, she looked in the small, murky mirror above the sink. The lower part of her face was a bright pink, but only from the rubbing, Hannah was convinced. It would disappear in a few minutes.

She turned to leave just as the door opened. Lucille was standing before her, a worried look on her face.

"Ah, Hannah. Miss Hyatt sent me in to see if you were all right. Ruth told her you had a coughing fit."

Hannah stared at Lucille. It was fate, she decided, the perfect chance to ask Lucille the question. Nobody would overhear. Nobody would interrupt, for only one person at a time was permitted to have the bathroom pass, a pink piece of paper that Lucille was now holding in her hand.

"You might be coming down with the measles or the chicken pox," Lucille said. "There's a sort of rash on your face. I've had both already, so don't worry."

She smiled sweetly, and Hannah felt a true affection for this kind person who seemed so concerned about Hannah's health. "Me, too," Hannah said. "When I was little."

"If you're feeling better, we should go back to the

classroom," Lucille advised, holding out her hand as if Hannah might faint from the strange illness she appeared to have.

"O.K., but first I want to ask you something." Hannah gulped, trying to remember the words she had had practiced.

"Oh? What?"

"Lucille, how come . . ." Hannah stopped. It would sound dumb after all, she decided suddenly. But Lucille was waiting. "Cynthia told me you were having a party, and I wondered—"

A quick frown came over Lucille's pretty face. "Oh, that Cynthia! She's very rude. That makes me very angry. She should never have mentioned the party to someone who isn't invited. I wish I hadn't asked her, either."

"Then she was right," Hannah whispered. "I'm not invited." She felt suddenly airy, as if she were floating somewhere above the bathroom sink.

"Oh, I'm sorry, Hannah. I hope you're not upset. It won't be much of a party, and, of course, I'd invite you if I could. But, I'm sorry." She took Hannah's arm lightly.

"Is it—is it because I'm Jewish?" Hannah asked.

Lucille looked relieved, and her face brightened with her smile. "Of course. You don't think I'd leave you out because I don't like you, do you? I like you very much."

Seventeen

"NAH, YOU DIDN'T HEAR HER RIGHT," ZACK said when Hannah told him about her conversation with Lucille.

"I did so. I heard every word she said," Hannah replied. But she was doubtful, too. It had been like a dream, a bad dream, and she wondered if it had occurred at all.

When the two girls had returned to Miss Hyatt's classroom that morning, Ruth had raised her eyebrows in question, but Hannah had ignored her. After school, she had run all the way home to avoid talking to anyone, and she had found Zack in the kitchen making a giant hard-boiled-egg sandwich.

"I mean, if she likes me so much, what difference would my religion make, right?" Hannah asked Zack for the third time.

Her brother was silently arranging lettuce and tomatoes atop the eggs, and Hannah was annoyed that he wasn't listening to her. "Zack—"

"Sh-h. I'm thinking," he said, continuing to work on his sandwich. He sighed deeply. Hannah watched him, wondering if his sigh was in admiration of the concoction he had created or for the difficulty of her question. "Lucille probably does like you, but not enough to change what she's been brought up to believe—that you just don't invite Jews into your home. Blame her parents for that," he said at last. "Listen, where does Ma keep the salt? Where is Ma, anyway?"

"At a meeting to talk about when the German refugees come," Hannah answered. She was surprised that she knew that answer, but her mother must have mentioned it last night. "I mean," she persisted, "it's like you and the team. You're probably one of the best players around and the dumb coach—"

"I think we've got that problem licked," Zack said casually.

"Really?" Hannah asked. For the first time that day, she had forgotten about Lucille. "How? Tell me."

"Well," he said slowly. "But you've got to promise not to tell the folks."

Hannah made an X motion with her finger on her chest. "Cross my heart and hope to die." She giggled. She had once done that in front of her mother, who didn't think it was funny and slapped Hannah's hand.

"Don't make fun of the *goyim* and don't make crosses," her mother had told her angrily.

But Zack laughed. "That gesture may be very appropriate," he said. "I'm all set to play on the Central Queens Y team. As a matter of fact, I've played a few games already."

"The Y team? You mean the YMCA?" Hannah asked. "They're Christian, Zack."

"So what? It's not like going to church or anything. And they have a swell gym, and my team is terrific—good guys—and a swell coach—Mr. MacShane. Lots of people—important people—come down and watch." He spoke quickly, as if he were trying to convince himself as well as Hannah.

"But, do they know—"

"It doesn't matter. All I did was sign a membership

card that says I'll uphold the Christian tradition. You know, Hannah," he continued, "it may be hard for you to believe after talking to that idiot Lucille this morning, but the Christian tradition is really all that stuff about 'Love Thy Neighbor.' "

"Humph." Hannah smirked.

"No, honest, it's the same thing as in Judaism. And I'm perfectly willing to love my neighbor if they'll let me play basketball."

"Then why don't you tell Ma and Pa?" Hannah asked.

"Well, you know. They're kind of old-fashioned."

Hannah shook her head in agreement. "O.K.," she said. "You know, I hope you become so famous that Coach whatever-his-name-is begs you to play on his team."

Zack winked. "That's the idea."

There was a knock on the kitchen door, and Zack quickly swallowed the last of his sandwich. "I don't want Ma to yell at me for spoiling my appetite," he whispered.

But it was not their mother. It was Ruth.

Hannah opened the door a crack and asked, "What do you want?"

"To talk to you, of course," Ruth said. "Let me in."

Hannah sighed and opened the door wider. "O.K., talk."

"Not me. You. What happened this morning? Why did you run home? I started to chase you, but you went too fast."

"I don't care to discuss it," Hannah said.

"That's not fair, Hannah," Ruth said, pouting. "It's terrible to know the beginning and not the end. Come on."

"Well, Lucille said she liked me very much."

"And the party? What about the party?"

"The party?" Hannah asked. "Oh, that. I never mentioned it."

Zack coughed loudly behind his sister.

"I don't believe you," Ruth said. "Cynthia told us you did."

"Oh, yeah? Where was she? Hiding in the toilet bowl?"

Ruth giggled.

"Oh, good, you're here," Bernice said, pushing through the door behind Ruth.

"Well?" she asked Ruth as if Hannah were not standing there. "What did she tell you?"

"Who invited you?" Hannah asked. "My mother," she said, looking directly at Bernice, "doesn't want everybody tracking up her floor."

But Bernice was too curious to protest Hannah's cruelty. "What happened?" she asked.

"Hey, what is this? Grand Central Station?" Zack asked as Billy Hermann's enormous body filled the doorway.

Ruth and Bernice turned quickly, startled to see him standing there. Hannah rolled her eyes and folded her arms.

"Yes?" she asked Billy. "Are you a member of the nosybody club?"

"Hi, Hannah. Hi, Zack. Hi, Ruth. Hi . . ." He looked at Bernice and wrinkled his brow.

"Bernice, dumbbell," she said, supplying her own name. "I only sat in front of you for six years. How could you forget my name?"

"You're a very forgettable person," Hannah said.

"Are you O.K.?" Billy asked Hannah. "I heard you was sick this morning."

"Hey, that's nice of you to inquire, Bill, old man," Zack said.

Billy smiled at him. "I can't stay. I got to go to work now, but I wanted to make sure Hannah, here, was O.K."

"Does he always come to visit you?" Ruth whispered. "I didn't know that."

"I'm fine," Hannah said. "Or at least I was until certain people dropped by."

"That's swell." Billy grinned. "Hey, listen. Did you change your mind about the party? I still got the note." He held out the invitation, now grimy and wrinkled.

Ruth put out her hand to take it, but Hannah grabbed it first and held it behind her back. "I told you, Billy, that it was . . ." She almost said "fake" but suddenly, looking at Ruth's and Bernice's eager faces, she changed her mind. "I'm thinking about it, Billy. I'll let you know."

"You mean you might?" Billy asked happily.

"Well," Hannah began, wondering how she could keep Ruth and Bernice from knowing the invitation was Cynthia's idea of a joke without encouraging poor Billy.

Zack waited for a moment to hear what his sister would say, then spoke up. "No, Bill, Hannah can't go. I heard my parents tell her she was too young to go to parties like that."

"And on Friday night, the Sabbath," Hannah added, wanting to hug her brother for his brilliance.

"Right," Zack said. He pulled her away from the others. "Leave well enough alone," he bent down and whispered. "Don't add any more reasons."

"Well, I guess I'll just go myself," Billy said. He looked very disappointed. "So long for now. I'm glad you're O.K." He waved halfheartedly, and they could hear his heavy footsteps walking through the dead leaves on the grass.

"I wouldn't have believed it if I hadn't heard it with my own ears," Ruth gasped. "So you *were* invited. That Cynthia! What a liar!"

"And all the time we thought that Lucille wouldn't invite anyone who was Jewish," Bernice said, shaking her head in amazement. "Well, now I know the real reason that *I* wasn't invited." She bent her head to indicate some sudden sad thought. "It's because—because I have no mother."

"Oh, for pity's sake, Bernice. What kind of reason would that be? What does having a mother got to do with anything?" Ruth asked angrily. "I have a mother and I wasn't invited."

"No," Bernice said in a quavering voice. "I know that's why. She probably thought that without a mother there would be nobody to help me look nice for the party and that I would come in my old skirt and blouse and my brown oxford shoes and—"

"Come on," Ruth said, grabbing Bernice by the arm. "That's enough. Let's go."

Bernice looked up, startled. Hannah was surprised, too. Ruth was always so gentle and sympathetic with Bernice. She really must be mad, Hannah thought happily.

When they left, Zack and Hannah burst out laughing. But, suddenly, Hannah stopped. "Hey, what about Billy? He said he was going, anyway. He didn't believe me about the fake note."

"Yeah, poor Bill," Zack agreed. He thought for a moment. "Well, don't worry. Irwin and I will try to head him off at the pass."

Eighteen

FOR SEVERAL DAYS, THE PHONE HAD NOT stopped ringing. Each time, Hannah raced to answer it, hoping that it was Lucille who had changed her mind and was indeed inviting Hannah to the party. There was not much time, Hannah realized, for the party was planned for the coming Friday night.

But it was never Lucille. It was always for her father. News had come that the Ackermanns' ship was due to arrive at any time now, and Mr. Brand would bolt down his dinner and race to the Hazelton Jewish Center for a committee meeting. Each time, he returned with the bad news. Hitler was playing games.

"He lets the ship sail, then calls it back. It must be going around in circles. First, Hitler claims they have hidden a criminal on board. I understand they searched everyone. Even shook out the blankets on a tiny baby. Then, that monster says the passengers have not paid enough fare, or someone has stolen an exit visa. He took several children as hostage until their parents found some more money. From where, I don't know. They probably had to sell the clothes on their backs. That's all most of them have, anyway."

"Well, at least they're alive, David," Mrs. Brand said. "Who knows what is happening to the poor Jews who can't afford to pay the blackmail Hitler demands."

"Nobody really knows," her husband said. "They disappear. Old men, young children. People who couldn't hurt a fly. His storm troopers arrest them for crimes against the state, whatever that means. Can you imagine a three-year-old child or an old lady in a wheelchair plotting to overthrow Hitler? He's a madman, a lunatic. He'll set fire to the world someday."

Once, late at night, Hannah heard her father's car drive away. The ship had arrived at midnight, someone had told him on the phone, and the Ackermanns were waiting on the dock, cold and alone and frightened.

Several hours later, he returned, weary and very angry. "It was a hoax. Somebody was playing a joke. There we were, Max Rabinowitz, the rabbi, and I, standing around like idiots, asking whoever passed by if they had seen the Ackermann family. There wasn't even a ship. People must have thought we were crazy or drunk."

"Who would do such a thing?" Mrs. Brand asked, and Hannah, who was just getting up for school, was upset to see her father with tears streaming from his red-rimmed eyes.

"Who knows? Except it was someone who knew about the Ackermanns."

"Not one of the congregation!" Mrs. Brand gasped.

"You think we're the only ones who know? There have been articles in the newspaper about our plans. No, it was some local Nazi," he said wearily. "Some *momzer* who doesn't want any more Jews in Hazelton."

"Dave, watch your language in front of the child," Mrs. Brand said. "Come, Hannah, hurry up."

"I know someone who plays jokes like that," Hannah said as her mother pushed a bowl of cereal in front of her. "Well, not exactly so mean, but mean enough."

"Really?" Mrs. Brand said, not paying much attention.

"It wasn't a girl on the phone, was it, Pa?" Hannah asked.

"A girl? Of course it was not a girl," he answered, trying to stifle a yawn.

Ruth was waiting for Hannah when she came out of the house.

"Where's what's-her-name?" Hannah asked.

"Sick," Ruth said, as if she doubted it. "Hannah, I wanted to ask you—"

"Skip it," Hannah said. "Listen, did you hear what happened last night?" She told Ruth about the hoax and her father's midnight trip. "You know who it probably was, don't you?"

Ruth shook her head no.

"That one, over there." She pointed her chin toward Cynthia who was standing back from Lucille obviously admiring her coat.

"Cynthia? That's nuts."

"Oh, yeah?" Hannah asked. "Well, she's been known to pull a few fast ones in her day." That's what they said in the movies about someone who wasn't quite honest.

"Like what?" Ruth wanted to know.

"Like . . ." Hannah stopped. She couldn't mention the invitation, of course. It would give away her secret. "Like she lied to you about me and the party, didn't she?"

"Oh, Hannah, that's not the same thing," Ruth argued. "That was little. This is big."

"Well, then, who else could it be?"

"If you want to know what I think, I think it was Arthur's father. Everybody knows that he's a Nazi. Remember when Arthur said you smell bad because you're

Jewish? He didn't make that up himself. He heard it at home. My father says that the apple does not fall far from the tree."

"Does your father make up sayings like that, too?" Hannah asked. "My mother's always . . ." She looked around quickly to see if Bernice had heard her, then sighed. It was a relief to have Bernice absent for a change.

"I'll bet that when your father drove away in the middle of the night, Mr. Marshall was standing at his window, smiling at his great joke," Ruth said.

Hannah shook her head, but it was not because she disagreed with Ruth. As a matter of fact, she didn't. But she was annoyed with herself for not having thought of it first. "It's a possibility," she admitted reluctantly. Nobody was supposed to be smarter than she was, especially not Ruth, Hannah thought, almost angrily. "Ask him," she suggested. "He's over there."

Ruth drew back, her round eyes growing rounder. "Never!"

"Then I will," Hannah said. She moved toward Arthur, hoping that Ruth would pull her back, but Ruth stood frozen.

"Be careful," Ruth said between clenched teeth.

"Hey, Arthur, come here," Hannah shouted.

"Why should I?"

"Because I have something to tell you."

"I'm not interested."

"It has something to do with your father."

"I'll be right back," she heard him tell the boy he was talking to. "What about my father?" he demanded, hands on his hips.

"How does he feel this morning?" Hannah asked sweetly.

"That's none of your business. Why do you want to know?"

"I mean, is he tired from all that phoning last night?"

Arthur's hand shot out and grabbed Hannah's coat lapels. "Were you looking in our windows, you sneaky Jew?"

Hannah was frightened, but tried not to show it. "N-no," she stuttered. Then, in amazement, she saw Arthur fly suddenly backward, clutching his stomach.

"Keep your hands off the girls," Billy was growling. "I don't never want to see you touch Hannah again. You hear me?"

A whistle blew, and Mrs. Wells was walking quickly toward them, faster than Hannah had ever seen her move. "What's going on here? Ah, Billy Hermann. I might have known. Are you all right, Arthur?" she asked, bending over the smaller boy.

"He punched me in the stomach," Arthur wailed.

"Nah, I just pushed him a little," Billy protested. "He was gonna hurt Hannah."

"I was not," Arthur shouted, forgetting his pain and jumping up and down.

"See?" Billy said. "He's all better already."

Mrs. Wells put her hand flat on Billy's chest, moving him slowly backward. "I told you what would happen if I caught you fighting in the schoolyard. I'd like to see you suspended. I'd like to see you thrown out of this school. You're not worth the money we spend on you." She finally had him backed against the fence, but only because Billy was willing to be pushed by the teacher. Otherwise, she would have moved him no farther than where he stood. "Miss Peterson will hear of this, and then we'll see."

She turned away, brushing off the hand that had touched Billy's jacket.

"He was only trying to—" Hannah began.

"Shut up! I saw what he was doing," Mrs. Wells shrieked.

When she had gone, Viola walked over to Hannah. "You shouldn't have started with her, Hannah. Can't you see it's one of her headache days?"

But Hannah wasn't listening. She had heard what she wanted from Arthur, and she could hardly wait to get home and tell her father.

"Was I right?" Ruth whispered.

"I hate to admit it, but you were right," Hannah whispered back.

Nineteen

———•••———

"AMEN," HANNAH MUMBLED WHEN HER father had finished the kiddush. She was angry at him, not the proper feeling for a Sabbath, she knew, but she couldn't help it. She watched him take a drink of wine following his blessing over it. The silver goblet he drank from reflected the flames of the Sabbath candles her mother had kindled just before sundown, and Hannah remembered how, when she was little, she had thought that only a king would drink from such a beautiful cup.

"Your father is a king," her mother had once told her. "He's king in this house."

Some king, Hannah thought. Kings were supposed to be brave and fight for truth and honor. But her father, it appeared, was a coward. He had refused to believe her when she had told him she knew who had made the phone call that had sent him rushing to the pier in the middle of the night.

"Did you see him?" her father had asked. "Are you positive? You know, Hannah, it's a sin to bear false witness, to lie about someone."

"But Arthur admitted it," Hannah had argued. "It was his father."

"You have no proof," Mr. Brand told her. "Do you?"

Hannah admitted she did not. Only the hint that Arthur had blurted out.

"So Mr. Marshall was on the phone that night. Maybe he was calling his mother to ask how she was feeling. Maybe he was calling a business acquaintance to find out about an order. Just because his son admits he was on the phone doesn't make him guilty of that cruel joke."

"It's what you call circumstantial evidence," Zack said. "But I'll bet Hannah is right."

"Never mind," Mr. Brand said. "We can only guess, and that's not evidence of any sort."

"Well, it was Ruth's idea, not mine," Hannah admitted weakly. If she couldn't have credit for solving the mystery, then she might as well let Ruth take the blame.

Zack was fidgeting in his chair. He played with the food his mother had placed before him and kept turning around to look at the clock on the buffet.

"You have a date or something?" Mrs. Brand asked.

"Not exactly," Zack muttered. "I promised Irwin I would come over with my math book."

"On Shabbas? Since when do you study on the Sabbath?" his father wanted to know.

"The Sabbath is supposed to be devoted to rest and study, Pa. What difference does it make if it's study of the Holy Books or of math?"

"I'm not going to quibble. If you promised Irwin, then go."

Zack let out a sigh of relief and finished his dinner. When he rose to put on his jacket, Hannah followed him.

"Be careful," she whispered. "Do you know where Lucille lives?" She told him the address again.

"Don't worry," Zack whispered back. "So long," he called to his parents, but his father stopped him.

"Didn't you forget something?" Mr. Brand asked. "Your math book, for instance?"

Zack slapped his forehead. "Boy, am I dumb." He ran upstairs, got the book, and left.

The plan was, Hannah knew, to meet Irwin at the corner and then follow the path they knew Billy would take to Lucille's. They hoped that he would be coming from home or else they might miss him. But if they did intercept him, they would merely explain, once again, and as slowly as they could so Billy would understand, that he and Hannah had not really been invited to the party and that if he went, it would be very embarrassing for him.

Hannah helped her mother clean up the kitchen and then sat down on the living-room sofa. She could see the clock on the buffet from where she sat, and the hands seemed to move unusually slowly. About half an hour, Zack had said the errand would take. Ten minutes to find Billy, five or ten to convince him, and then return home. It was almost that time now, Hannah saw, and she tapped her foot impatiently against the coffee table.

Her father was snoring in the corner chair, and her mother's head was nodding slower and slower as she listened to the evening news on the radio. Hannah was glad her parents were not as religious as Shirley's about turning on the radio or the lights on the Sabbath. It was considered "work" to turn the dial or flick the switch, and very observant Jews did neither. They didn't ride, handle money, write, or cook—everything had to be prepared before sundown on Friday night. For the twenty-four hours until sundown on Saturday, Shirley's mother kept a low flame on the stove, over which a pot of thick soup bubbled softly. It was delicious soup, Hannah remembered, full of meat and vegetables, which she and Shirley had often eaten with thick slices of home-baked challah, for their Saturday lunch. If she had closed her eyes right now, she was sure she could remember the aroma.

"No," she said aloud, and jumped up to wake herself. "Don't fall asleep." Her parents had not stirred. Hannah went into the kitchen to check the clock over the sink. "What is he doing?" she wondered. Probably he went back to Irwin's after meeting Billy, she decided. Or, maybe, Lucille had seen him and invited him in. That would be funny, Hannah thought.

She tiptoed back into the living room and peered down at her parents. Fast asleep. Carefully, she took her coat from the closet, keeping one eye on her parents, and slowly opened the door. If they awoke, she would tell them she was going for a walk. Once outside, she raced down the block and reached Lucille's street. Two figures were moving toward her whom she recognized immediately.

"Hannah, what are you doing here! Go home," Zack said angrily.

"What happened? Where's Billy? Did you convince him?" she asked, trying to catch her breath.

"It was like pulling teeth," Irwin muttered. "Boy, is he stubborn."

"And mad," Zack added. "I think he wanted to strangle Cynthia."

"Did you see the party?" Hannah asked. "Were they dancing? What did they have to eat?"

Before Zack could reply, a loud crash sounded behind them. Glass breaking and then the sound of running feet. Billy almost collided with them.

"Come on," he whispered, grabbing Zack's arm. "Let's beat it."

"Wha . . . ?" Irwin asked.

But Billy continued running alone, turning around once to wave them to hurry. "Come on," he shouted hoarsely.

There was a sudden brightness as the outside lights were turned on and faces appeared in Lucille's doorway. "There they are," someone called. "Grab them. They're the ones who broke the window."

"Call the police," a woman's voice said. Zack, Hannah, and Irwin watched the activity in amazement.

They stood frozen as several figures moved toward them.

"Lucille, come in the house," the woman's voice called. "Those people are dangerous."

"Who are they talking about?" Hannah asked, moving closer to Zack.

"I don't know," Zack answered. "I don't think they saw Billy."

"I think," Irwin said, as a stocky man with a pipe in his mouth came closer, "they're talking about us."

Twenty

AS THE POLICE CAR PULLED UP TO THE curb, the crowd grew larger.

"Here they are, officers," the man with the pipe said. "Caught red-handed."

"I knew it," Arthur shouted. "I knew it would be those Jews who live next door to me. I could smell them a mile away."

"All right, let's have none of that," a very tall policeman said. "Let's have some facts in this matter."

Hannah could see Lucille and Cynthia standing at the back edge of the crowd. She wondered if they could see her, too.

"My name is Travis, Lawrence Travis, officer," the man with the pipe said. "And my daughter was giving this small party for her friends and suddenly a rock crashed through our living-room window. These youngsters were the only people around. They must have thrown it."

"No," Zack protested. "We were only walking by—"

"First, some important information," the policeman said. "Was anyone hurt?"

"No—" Mr. Travis began, but his wife interrupted.

"A vase, a family heirloom," she said. "Smashed to bits. It is irreplaceable."

"But nobody was hurt, right?" the other policeman asked politely.

"Well, no," Mrs. Travis admitted. "But the vase—it belonged to my great-grandmother."

The tall policeman turned away from her. He gently moved Hannah, Zack, and Irwin into the light of the street lamp. "Well, now, what have we here? Don't I know you?"

"Mr. MacShane," Zack gasped.

"Zachary Brand!" the policeman responded. "Did you do this?"

"No, Mr. MacShane, honest."

"Did he?" the policeman asked, pointing at Irwin.

"None of us did it," Zack answered. He looked at Irwin, who was staring blankly at the lamppost, unable to speak.

"And this little girl?"

"Me?" Hannah squeaked. "I—"

"All right. Where do you live?"

"Not around here," Arthur said. "They live near me, and it's far from here."

"Not that far," Hannah muttered.

"But they don't live on this block, and the only reason they were here was to make trouble," Arthur insisted.

"Well, young fellow," Officer MacShane said, "you seem to know an awful lot about this situation. Would you like to make a statement for the record? As an eyewitness?" He whipped out a pad and pencil and began writing.

"No," Arthur shrieked. "I didn't see anything. I don't know anything." He moved backward into the crowd.

"Then I advise you to be quiet," Officer MacShane

said. He turned to Mr. Travis. "Would you like to swear out a complaint, sir?"

"Of course," Lucille's father said.

"First let me talk to them alone," the policeman said. "As it happens, Mr. Travis, I know this young man. I work with him at the YMCA. He's a fine boy. You can tell a boy's character when you see him work with a team."

"Oh?" Mr. Travis asked. "Very well. But I'll expect to hear from you."

"Indeed you will," Officer MacShane said. "O.K. now, everyone break it up. Go back inside."

The other policeman waved his hands to scatter the crowd.

"Hannah, I'm shocked," Cynthia called back over her shoulder. "Aren't you, Lucille, dear?"

Hannah's teeth had begun to chatter. She felt cold and frightened as the two policemen urged them gently toward the police car.

"Let's sit in here. It's warmer," Officer MacShane said.

Slowly, the three of them followed the policemen and huddled in the back seat of the car.

"So," Officer MacShane began, "let's hear your story, Zack."

Zack told him what had happened, about the invitation to the party and how they had tried to stop "a boy" from being embarrassed.

Had they seen this "boy" throw the rock, the policemen wanted to know?

No, they admitted. They had only heard the crash of glass as they were walking away from the Travis house.

"Sounds pretty fishy to me," the other policeman said. "Where is this mysterious boy you're talking about?"

"He ran away," Hannah blurted out, then covered her mouth with her hand. Better keep quiet, she thought.

"Now, Zack, I'd like you to tell me the name of this person," Officer MacShane said kindly. "It's no pleasure to be a tattletale, but if you don't give me his name, I have no choice but to think that there is no such person." He studied the three faces in the back seat for a moment. "And that would leave only one conclusion. That you were the perpetrators."

"The what?" Hannah asked.

"The individuals who committed this—this crime," the policeman explained.

"Mr. MacShane, I—I can't. He's a dumb kid who just lost his temper. He didn't mean any harm. He was just mad because Lucille Travis and her friends were playing a joke on my sister." Zack pointed to Hannah.

"Not Lucille," Hannah said quickly. "Only Cynthia. Lucille wouldn't do such a thing."

"You understand," Officer MacShane said, as if he had been thinking about it for a while, "that you were mighty lucky. That rock could have really hurt somebody, sent them to the hospital—"

"But it didn't," Zack protested.

"—and then, we'd have a possible felony on our hands," Officer MacShane continued. "Very, very serious."

"But, only a vase—" Hannah whispered.

"Yes, fortunately, only a vase." Officer MacShane nodded grimly. "And a window. Don't forget that."

"What are you going to do?" Zack asked.

The policeman sighed and studied the three huddled figures in the back seat. "Well," he said, "I could book you for vandalism—"

Hannah gasped. That sounded worse than felony.

"But, knowing Zack here as I do, I'm going to give you the benefit of the doubt. I think he's trustworthy enough to be released in his own recognizance."

"Oh, he is, he is," Hannah insisted, although she had no idea what this meant.

"So, against all regulations, I'll let you go for the moment. For some dumb reason, I believe you. Go home and sleep on it, and tomorrow you can come down to the station house and make a statement. Promise?"

Hannah, Zack, and Irwin nodded as they climbed out of the car.

Officer MacShane leaned out the window and beckoned Zack to move closer. "I hope you realize, Zack, that as there were no eyewitnesses to this vandalism, it may be hard to press charges against you. But if you don't come up with that name tomorrow—well, the circumstantial evidence is pretty overwhelming—I'll undoubtedly have to take you off the team." He rolled up the window as the car drove away.

Twenty-one

"HE AIN'T HERE," THE RED-FACED MAN SAID,
his breath sitting on the cold air like a small cloud. He
was dressed in what was once a heavy woolen sweater,
but now looked like a bowl of dark gray spaghetti because there were so many long, loose strings of yarn
hanging from it. The man continued to load his arms
from the pile of rough logs beside his door, and Hannah waited, hoping he would say something else. She
hopped up and down to keep warm while the man
worked. "Will he come back soon?" she asked.

The man glanced at her and went into the house.
Hannah turned away and began to walk back home. It
was barely eight o'clock, but she had wanted to find
Billy before Zack had a chance to go to the police station. Her house had been warm and silent as she left,
her parents and Zack still fast asleep. But they would be
up soon because her father would want to go to the Sabbath morning service at the synagogue. She had thought
about the problem half the night and then could barely
sleep when the answer came to her. Billy would confess.
Zack would have nothing more to do with it, and that
would be the end of that. But she would have to let
Billy know.

"Hey, kid, wait a minute," the man who was apparently Billy's father called out. Hannah ran back toward

him. "See if you can make this out," Mr. Hermann said, handing Hannah a sheet of lined paper that had been ripped out of a notebook.

I done something bad. Don't wurry. I got munny from my job. Your son William Hermann.

Hannah read it twice and handed it back to Billy's father.

"You know something about this?" he asked, as if he were afraid she might.

"Well . . ." Hannah said. She wondered if Mr. Hermann would be angry or relieved if she told him the story.

"He was trying real hard to be a good boy," the man said. "He was making friends and everything. He told me about a girl in his class who was nice to him. And he was even invited to a party. The first one he was ever invited to." He studied Hannah's face for a moment. "Is that where it happened? Did he do something bad at the party?" His face wrinkled up, and Hannah wasn't sure if he was about to cry.

"Sort of," Hannah mumbled. "I mean, I wasn't there. I only heard."

"Heard what?" Mr. Hermann slowly rubbed a knuckle against his lips. Reluctantly, Hannah changed her mind about telling him. She felt sorry for Mr. Hermann who seemed so pleased that Billy was making friends at last. "Nothing. Just that he—he was—well, he tripped and knocked over Mrs. Travis's vase."

A broad smile came over Mr. Hermann's face. "Is that all? Oh, I mean, it's too bad about the vase, but it was an accident, wasn't it? It could happen to anyone, couldn't it? Billy's so big, he's really clumsy. But, that wasn't anything bad, was it?"

"Oh no," said Hannah uncertainly.

"But this note. He says he done something bad." He frowned and looked at the paper again. It reminded

Hannah of Billy's reading Cynthia's make-believe invitation, and she shivered with hatred at the girl.

"Well, I suppose he felt really sorry. Maybe he went out to buy another vase. Doesn't it say something about money?" Hannah pointed to the words on the note.

"That's it!" Mr. Hermann said. "That's what he done. He's probably looking all over town for a new vase." He smiled at Hannah. "You know, that's really nice of him, don't you think? It shows he has good manners. Me and my wife done a good job, after all, bringing him up, right?"

"Right," Hannah said weakly. "Well, I have to go." She turned once more for home.

"Hey, Kate," she heard Mr. Hermann calling to someone in the house, "it's O.K., Billy ain't really in trouble." The door slammed behind him.

She wondered why it had not occurred to Billy's father to ask what she was doing there so early in the morning.

"Thank God," Mrs. Brand yelled as Hannah walked in the door. "I thought you were kidnapped. Where were you? Zack was afraid you had run away."

Hannah looked at her brother, whose eyes were drooping. She supposed he had not slept much either.

"Zachary, you'll fall into your cereal. Sit up," Mrs. Brand said. "So, young lady, where were you?"

"I took a walk," Hannah said.

"A walk? Every time I fall asleep, you take a walk. Last night, and now this morning. You should have legs like a horse if you keep this up."

Zack chuckled in spite of his weariness. But when his mother turned back to the stove, he whispered, "Where were you?"

Hannah set her finger to her lips. "I'll tell you later," she whispered back.

Upstairs, as Zack finished dressing, she told him.

Her brother looked disappointed. "I hope he hasn't disappeared for good. That would really fix my wagon." "Well, what are you going to do?" Hannah asked. "I'll think about it in *shul*. Maybe I'll have a divine revelation or something. Boy, I wish they still had a few miracles around."

Her father didn't insist that Hannah come to services with them. He said she looked tired and should rest. She helped her mother straighten up the house and then wondered whether she should walk over to Ruth's. She was anxious to know if anybody else had heard about last night.

"Ma," she shouted. "I'm going over to Ruth's. Did you hear me? I don't want you to say I didn't tell you." "Go, go," her mother called back. "Be home soon."

As she stood on the porch buttoning her coat, Arthur came out of his front door.

"What are you doing here?" he asked. "I thought you'd be in jail."

"Shut up," Hannah sneered. "You're the one who should be in jail. With your father, the midnight phone caller."

"Nyah, nyah," Arthur taunted. "Try and prove something."

"I won't have to," Hannah said. "Here come the police to take you away." She watched the police car drive slowly down the block, and drew in her breath. "Speak of the devil and the devil appears," she said to herself.

"They're coming for you," Arthur said, but not quite certain.

"Oh, no. They're coming for you," Hannah replied, equally uncertain.

But they stopped in front of neither house. They were parking across the street, in front of Cynthia's. She and

Arthur stood in amazement as Officer MacShane and his partner walked up the steps to the Sherwoods' front door. Within a few minutes, they came out again, neither of them smiling. They got into the car and drove off.

"Probably went to get some handcuffs," Arthur said.

"Probably to get a straitjacket for you and your father," Hannah sneered. "Only crazy people are Nazis."

"Oh yeah? You think Hitler is crazy? As soon as he gets here, you'll be in trouble. Big trouble."

"Really? I didn't know Hitler was coming to America," Hannah said. "Did your father invite him?"

"He doesn't have to. He goes wherever he wants to, and when he gets here, he's going to make my father a general in his army."

Hannah spit. She wished she could reach Arthur, but he was too far away.

"Spitting. Beautiful," Mrs. Brand said behind her. "I'm glad you're still here. Come in, please, madame who spits and gets phone calls from the police."

"I knew it," Arthur shouted. "They're after you."

Mrs. Brand stepped out farther onto the porch to see who had spoken. "Oh, that one," she said to Hannah. "It's no wonder you spit."

"Is this for me or for Zack?" Hannah asked before she picked up the receiver.

"The officer asked for Zack first, but he said he'll settle for you. What's going on, my daughter, what does he want?"

Hannah waved her mother to silence as she whispered hello.

"Hannah, tell your brother, please, that he doesn't have to come down here. We have the name of the boy. Hello? Do you hear me?" Officer MacShane asked.

"How—how did you find out?" Hannah asked.

"We have ways. I knew my boy Zachary couldn't do such a thing. I'll see him tomorrow afternoon at practice. Tell him that, too."

"Mr. MacShane, is Billy in jail?"

For a moment, there was no answer. "Not yet. We've yet to find him, but he'll turn up."

"He really is a nice boy, Mr.—" Hannah started to add, but the phone was dead.

Mrs. Brand looked as if she were about to burst. "So, now? Speak!"

"I want to wait until Zack comes back," Hannah said.

"Listen, you're not too big to give a good smack across the mouth. Talk!"

"I don't know the whole story, Ma. I wasn't there the whole time when Zack and Irwin were talking to Billy."

"Billy? Who's Billy? And where does Irwin fit in?" Mrs. Brand's face was getting red, and she jumped up to grab Hannah by the shoulders.

"Lillie, what's going on?" Mr. Brand asked as he and Zack entered the house. "That's a lovely Shabbas greeting to come home to—my wife shaking her daughter's *kishkas* out."

Mrs. Brand sat down again and fanned herself with her hand. "David, if you knew what was going on here this morning. Police—"

"Police?" Mr. Brand yelled. "What? Who?"

"Hey, Zack, it's O.K. Your divine revelation came true." Hannah hugged her brother happily.

"Oh, I can't stand another minute, David. What is she saying?" Mrs. Brand wailed.

"Quiet!" Zack shouted. "Hannah, are you sure?"

Hannah nodded and told him Officer MacShane's message.

"That's swell, but how did he find out?" Zack slapped his forehead. "Irwin. He must have come to and told."

"Irwin was knocked unconscious?" Mr. Brand asked.

"It wasn't Irwin. I think it was Cynthia," Hannah said. "The police were at her house this morning."

"Cynthia?" Mrs. Brand asked. "What kind of a neighborhood is this, anyway?"

Finally, everyone stopped talking, and Zack told his parents about the night before. When he had finished, Mr. and Mrs. Brand still seemed bewildered.

"One more thing. Mr. MacShane reminded you about practice tomorrow," Hannah said.

"Mr. MacShane is the policeman, right?" Mrs. Brand asked suspiciously. "What kind of practice?"

"He's a volunteer coach at the YMCA," Zack said. "I think it's pretty swell of him to spend his spare time coaching the basketball team there."

"And what do you have to do with the YMCA?" Mrs. Brand asked. "Every time you answer a question, it leads to another one."

"You'd better tell them, Zack," Hannah said.

Her brother agreed.

"Good. Now, do we know everything? From now on, no more secrets, no more surprises, please." Mr. Brand pulled out a handkerchief from his pocket and wiped his forehead.

"Are we ready for lunch?" Mrs. Brand asked. "Hannah, set the table. I made some nice soup."

"As good as Mrs. Levine's?" Hannah rubbed her stomach.

"Ah, speaking of the Levines, Hannah, here is today's mail," Mr. Brand said, handing his daughter an envelope. "A letter from Shirley."

Twenty-two

FOR TWO WHOLE WEEKS, BILLY HAD NOT been in school. Each morning, a new rumor about his absence circulated among the eighth grade. Someone said he had been found hiding at the lumberyard near the railroad tracks where he worked. Walter Sorg told the class that he had caught a glimpse of Billy, buried deep in blankets, riding by in a speeding ambulance.

Lucille slipped Hannah a note apologizing for thinking that Hannah had been involved in the window-breaking, with a postscript saying that the police had told her father that Billy had not yet been caught.

"I know that," Hannah wrote back. "Mr. MacShane told my brother. They're very good friends."

Hannah found herself suddenly very popular. She was the only one in the class who knew the story from the beginning, and for the moment she became an expert on Billy, the police, and any other subject that came up.

"You know who's the most worried?" Viola asked. "Mrs. Wells. The police asked her about Billy. They told her they heard that she didn't like him."

"Oh, but that wouldn't have anything to do with it. Lots of teachers don't like Billy," Consuelo said. "He never does his homework."

"And he's always sleeping in class," Ruth added.

"Yeah," Viola said, "but that's not the whole reason with Mrs. Wells."

Hannah put her hands on her hips and said, in a sneering voice, "Tell us already, if you know so much. You've been hinting at some deep, dark secret for ages." She was sure, though, that Viola couldn't know as much as she did.

"O.K., but don't tell anyone you heard it from me. Remember, Consuelo, in the sixth grade when Mrs. Wells caught Billy looking in her handbag?"

Consuelo drew in a deep breath, and her big brown eyes blinked rapidly. "Do I? Mrs. Wells said Billy was trying to steal her money."

"I don't know, maybe he was," Viola whispered. "But he found something else. I saw it, too."

"What? What?" Hannah asked impatiently.

"A flask," Viola answered.

"A flask? What's that?" Hannah asked.

"Boy, I thought you knew everything," Viola said. "A flask is a skinny bottle you keep whiskey in. I ought to know. My mother . . ." She stopped. "Well, never mind."

"Mrs. Wells drinks whiskey?" Hannah shook her head no. "Only bums on the street corners drink whiskey. Teachers don't."

"Then why do you think she has so many headaches? Why do you think she didn't come to school for the first two weeks? Whiskey does that. I ought to know."

"O.K., I believe you," Hannah mumbled. "So that's why she's so anxious for Billy to be kicked out. She's afraid he might tell."

"And if the police get him, he might tell them," Consuelo said. "I get it now."

Once, after arithmetic class, Mrs. Wells held Hannah back from leaving and asked her to sit down. "I'll give you an excuse for your next period," she said.

Hannah waited for the teacher to say something about her grades or her behavior or whatever else she was always complaining about. Instead, she asked Hannah if there was any news about Billy. When Hannah told her there was nothing new, Mrs. Wells patted her upper lip with her handkerchief.

"Perhaps I've been too harsh with him. You know, he's not quite"—she made a circle with her finger next to her forehead—"all there."

"You mean Billy is crazy?" Hannah asked. "Oh, no, Mrs. Wells, he's just a little slow. But don't worry. I'm sure he won't tell about the—little bottle." She sat there smiling at the teacher innocently, and watched her turn a deep red. She was sure Mrs. Wells would not be mean to her anymore.

"You may go!" Mrs. Wells said, finally finding her voice. She scribbled something on a piece of paper, the excuse she had promised Hannah for being late to her next class, and gave Hannah a push toward the door.

But, after a time, Billy's disappearance was no longer of much interest. There were just so many guesses that could be made, and each one had proved to lead nowhere. Hannah was disappointed that her classmates had stopped asking her opinion and tried, every now and then, to bring up the subject.

"I hope he's back in time for Christmas," she told Ruth. "I know how his parents must feel."

"Let's talk about something else. I'm sick of the whole thing," Ruth answered.

"Anyway," Bernice added, "you don't know any more than we do, so there."

"That's what you think," Hannah said, trying to sound as if she knew much more, but Ruth merely yawned.

"I bet Twin Ponds will be frozen soon, and I'm getting ice skates for Hanukkah," she said.

"I don't get presents," Hannah said. "Only Christians get presents. I'm getting money, Hanukkah *gelt*. I'm going to use it to take Shirley to the movies and to a restaurant."

"Shirley? Your friend from the Bronx? You didn't tell me she was coming," Ruth said.

This time it was Hannah who yawned. "I suppose it slipped my mind in all the excitement about Billy." She waited to see if Ruth would say something about the missing boy, but she didn't. "I got a letter from her a few weeks ago, on the very day after Billy disappeared."

"Boy, we'll have lots of visitors soon," Ruth said. "Shirley, and the Ackermanns, and . . ." Those were all she could think of.

"If the Ackermanns ever show up," Hannah said.

"Oh, didn't you know? They're coming, definitely. My father heard—"

"I was thinking," Hannah said. "Isn't it funny that with all that stuff going on in the world that nobody ever mentions it in school? I mean, in history or whatever. Not a word. It is history, you know."

"I'm glad," Bernice mumbled. "I don't want everybody talking about Jews and stuff. It makes me feel scrunchy inside. Even when I hear it on the radio."

"Me, too," Ruth said.

"Hey," Bernice whispered. "Look who's walking behind us."

The other two girls turned around.

"Cynthia, the red-headed rat," Hannah said. "And all

alone. What's the matter, Cynthia?" she called over her shoulder. "Nobody to walk with you?" She turned back to Ruth and Bernice. "Serves her right. It's all her fault, you know, about Billy. If she hadn't written that note—"

"Please," Ruth begged, "no more about Billy." She sighed with relief as they reached the corner of her and Bernice's street. "See you, Hannah. Come on, Bernice. I'm freezing."

Hannah walked on slowly, hoping that Cynthia would try to catch up to her. She was sure that Cynthia would be willing to discuss the Billy situation, or anything else Hannah wanted to talk about. Nobody had spoken to Cynthia for weeks. Lucille had snubbed her, and Consuelo and Viola had therefore done the same thing.

Hannah decided to be generous and permit Cynthia to listen to her. She turned around once more, but as slowly as Hannah walked, so did Cynthia.

"Don't be afraid. I won't bite you," Hannah said.

"If you do, I'll get rabies," Cynthia sneered.

"Listen, Cynthia. You're the one everybody's mad at, not me," Hannah said. That Cynthia had some nerve being nasty when she, Hannah, was willing to talk to her. "You're to blame for all this."

"All what?" Cynthia asked, gazing around.

"You know what I'm talking about. Billy."

Suddenly, Cynthia put on a burst of speed and caught up to Hannah. "Well," she said, "I like that! If you hadn't been so dumb, Hannah, you would have known that invitation was a joke. And so would that dumb Billy. Boy, is he dumb."

"Dumb, dumb, dumb. Is that your favorite new word? Do you like it better than 'outfit'?" Hannah asked.

"Anyway, I hope 'dumb Billy' is still alive." She looked at Cynthia from beneath her lashes. "Because, if he isn't, you killed him."

Cynthia gasped. "Oh, that's a terrible thing to say! Of course he's alive. He's just hiding somewhere."

"All this time? Come on, I happen to think—"

"I don't care what you think," Cynthia screamed and ran across the street toward her house.

"Wow, what was that all about? I think she's crying," Zack said as he came up behind his sister, his arms loaded with books. "You haven't said anything mean to her, have you?"

"Humph," Hannah snorted. "Why not? She was mean to me."

"Because two wrongs don't make a right. Don't stoop to her level, Hannah. I liked you better the way you were."

"Before when?"

"Before you became such a big shot about this Billy business." He smiled at her, but Hannah could see he was serious.

"How have I changed?" Hannah asked. The idea that Zack would stop liking her made her unhappy.

"Well," he said, pretending he was thinking hard, "you haven't asked to borrow my eraser lately. Oh, and you don't have a chocolate mustache after drinking cocoa anymore. That used to be cute, Hannah. You shouldn't have learned to use a napkin. It changed your whole personality."

Hannah giggled. Zack couldn't stay angry for long.

Twenty-three

"AT LAST!" MR. BRAND SAID. HE RAISED both his arms as if to hug Dr. Ackermann, but hesitated and, instead, shook his hand very hard. Tears filled the eyes of both men, as they had the eyes of everyone else during the welcoming ceremonies for the German family.

There had been speeches and prayers, and the small auditorium of the synagogue hummed with whispers and excitement.

"They are so thin," Mrs. Brand said when she first saw the family—the tall, gray-haired doctor, his equally tall wife, and their two daughters, Wilma, who had surprisingly pink cheeks, and blond Trudie.

Now they stood in a reception line mumbling *"Danke schoen"* to everyone who passed by regardless of what was said to them.

"I guess they don't speak English," Hannah whispered to Ruth and Bernice, who were standing behind her.

"We'll have to teach them, I mean, the younger one, Trudie. She'll be in our class," Ruth said.

"For what's left of the year," Hannah replied. "She better learn fast." Now it was her turn to greet the Ackermanns, and Hannah shook each hand, feeling the bony dryness of Trudie's fingers in hers. She could think of nothing to say and merely nodded.

Behind her, Ruth was bubbling about how joyous Hanukkah would be this year for the Hazelton Jewish community, repeating almost word for word the rabbi's speech. Hannah pulled her by the arm.

"You're holding everyone up," she whispered. How come Ruth could think of what to say and she could not, she wondered. "Let's get something to drink."

They moved to the refreshment table and pushed their way toward the punch and cookies. The handshaking was over, and the Ackermanns were surrounded by people anxious to be the first to invite them for dinner.

At the edge of the throng, Trudie stood alone, twisting a handkerchief in her hands.

"I think she's looking at us," Bernice whispered. "Let's go back and talk to her."

"What for? I can't speak German," Hannah said.

"We'll try. Come on. She's standing all by herself. It's a good chance."

Slowly, the three girls moved toward Trudie, but when they reached her, Ruth and Bernice seemed dumbstruck. They opened their mouths, but no words came out.

"Ah, you big shots," Hannah muttered. She smiled at Trudie. "Me Hannah," she said, imitating a cavalry officer talking to an Indian chief in a movie she had seen. "This Ruth and this Bernice. You Trudie."

The girl stared at her with wide blue eyes.

"Us friends," Hannah continued, putting her arms around Ruth and Bernice. "You want be our friend, too?"

"That my father. That my mother. They help you get to America in big boat sail over deep water," Ruth added, suddenly catching on. She made a waving motion with her hand and was about to pretend she was seasick when Trudie smiled.

"*Ya*, I have met them. Your parents, too, Hannah. And yours?" She nodded toward Bernice and looked around.

"Her only have one parent. Her mother dead many moons," Hannah said. She sniffed and screwed up her face to show Trudie she was saying something sad.

"Ach, I am so sorry," Trudie said, patting Bernice's hand.

"In case you haven't noticed," Mr. Brand interrupted, "Trudie speaks English very well."

"What?" Hannah asked. "Oh, yeah, that's right. We just heard her." She could feel her face grow hot, and she giggled with embarrassment.

"These girls will be in your class," Mrs. Brand told Trudie. "I'm sure you'll have a lot to say to one another."

"Oh, yes," Ruth said, and she began a long monologue on Spring Street School, the teachers, the students, the neighborhood, and the fact that the girls had to make their own graduation dresses.

"Come, Trudie, we must go now," Dr. Ackermann interrupted. "I'm glad you have met children your own age." He made a small bow to the girls. "You will please excuse us now, ladies. It has been an exciting but tiring experience."

Trudie turned and looked at Hannah over her shoulder. "*Auf Wiedersehen*," she called.

"See you around," Hannah called back.

"They don't look so bad," Ruth said. "I mean, for all the things that happened to them."

"I thought they looked sad. I know what it is to lose everything . . ." Bernice said with a sigh.

"Oh, shut up, Bernice. You don't know anything," Hannah said. But she agreed with Ruth. She had expected to see four shriveled-up, shivering people with dark circles around their eyes and ragged clothing. Instead, the Ackermanns stood straight and smiled.

"They put on a good act," Zack said when Hannah pointed this out to him. "But, way down deep, I'm sure there's quite a bit of shriveling up."

Twenty-four

HANNAH TOOK HER TIME GETTING DRESSED. If she wasn't ready, her father would have to drive to the railroad station alone, which would mean fifteen minutes less of Shirley. What would they talk about after all this time? It was four months since her family had moved to Hazelton, but it seemed as though she had lived here all her life.

She stared out her bedroom window at the street below. It was beautiful, even prettier than it had been in the summer when the trees lining Dudley Road had made a bridge from one side to the other. Prettier even than in the fall when those same trees were gold and red. Now, they were bare, but the snow that had been falling for two days covered the sidewalk and the front yards, sparkling white, not like in the Bronx where it turned to dirty gray slush almost immediately.

On many of the front doors along the street, Christmas wreaths were hanging, their red bows and pine cones making the "season bright," as the Christmas songs said. Hannah wished, for the first time, that they could hang a wreath on their door. What would it mean, she had asked her parents. That they were celebrating the birth of Christ? That was ridiculous. It would only mean that their door would be as pretty as Cynthia's or Arthur's or the others.

Even more than a wreath, Hannah wanted a Christmas tree. At night, she could see Cynthia's tree gleaming with candles and silver balls through the window. She supposed Arthur's was just as nice, but lately, the Marshalls had kept their shades down so nobody could see inside.

Hannah had hoped that Lucille or Consuelo or somebody would invite her to their homes to help trim their trees, or at least look at them up close. But nobody had.

Oh, they had one in school, a scraggly tree whose lower branches were rusty brown and whose decorations were colored-paper chains made by the kindergarten kids. That wasn't the same.

Ruth had said the school had no right to put a tree in the school's front hall, that it was a symbol of a Christian holiday and that the schools were for everybody, even for people who didn't celebrate Christmas. She had said the same thing about singing carols in assembly.

"Why should Mrs. Wells get mad if I don't sing about Little Lord Jesus or the brownyon virgin?" she asked indignantly. "Whatever that is."

"The 'brownyon virgin'?" Hannah had repeated.

"Oh, come on, Hannah. 'Brownyon virgin, mother and child . . .' " she sang.

Hannah smirked. "You mean 'Round yon Virgin,' not 'brownyon.' "

"Well, whatever. I don't want to sing about it," Ruth said.

"Don't tell me. Tell Mrs. Wells or Miss Peterson," Hannah suggested.

"I can't. They'd get mad. And it would only start trouble."

"Then just shut up about it," Hannah said. But, as usual, she secretly agreed with Ruth. It made her uncomfortable, too, to sing about "our dear Savior's birth." She had told her father, too, pretending that it had been her idea, not Ruth's.

"It's a Christian world, Hannah. It won't kill you to sing," Mr. Brand had said.

Hannah smoothed out the dresser scarf Shirley had given her and looked in the mirror. "Gorgeous," she said aloud.

Her father was waiting with his hat and coat on and carrying Hannah's galoshes in one hand. "Put them on," he said. "Your mother's orders."

The road was slippery, and her father drove very slowly. Now Hannah was worried they would be late and wished she hadn't dawdled. They arrived at the tiny station just as the train was pulling in.

"I see her," Hannah shouted, relieved that she recognized her old friend. "Shirl, hey, Shirl."

Shirley could barely walk, she was so loaded down with packages and luggage. Mr. Brand took as many as he could carry, and Hannah grabbed at the small suitcase.

"Gee, it's good to see you," Hannah said, surprised that she meant it. "Go slow, Pa, so that Shirley can see Hazelton."

"It's so quiet, Hannah. How can you stand it?" Shirley peered out the back window. "Gee, you have a lot of *goyim* here," she said. "I counted thirty-seven Christmas wreaths already."

"Yes, it's not quite like Tremont Avenue," Mr. Brand said, laughing. "Ah, there's your mother, Hannah, waiting and probably worrying that Shirley got lost."

"Come in, come in," Mrs. Brand called. "I was worried you got lost. Zachary, help with the suitcases. What are all these bundles? Did your mother think we wouldn't have any food out here?"

"Presents," Shirley said. "For everybody."

"We'll put them under our tree." Hannah laughed, but Shirley looked startled.

"Oh, you're kidding," she said. "I thought maybe you really changed."

"Not that much," Mrs. Brand said, "even though some people in this house would like it. All right, run upstairs with Hannah and get settled. Then we'll have lunch. Hannah, your friends have been here already. I sent them away."

"They're all dying to meet you, Shirl," Hannah said, as they went upstairs.

"Are they as much fun as Eli and everybody?" Shirley asked. She looked around. "Your room is nice, Hannah, but I liked the one in the apartment better. And the snow, doesn't it make you squint all the time? It's so shiny."

"It's better than ugly old slush," Hannah said, growing annoyed.

"When your friends come, do they have to walk through the cold? Remember how even though it rained or snowed, we could just go down the stairs or through the hall and visit each other?"

"See for yourself," Hannah said, as she heard voices outside.

They came, just as they had the first time, trooping through the backyard, Bernice dragging Teddy, who slipped on the path and began to cry.

"Wipe your nose," Reva said.

"It'll freeze," Carol added.

They stood at the back door, making snowballs and

shouting until Hannah and Shirley came outside. Then they waited to be introduced, which Hannah did quickly. "There's one more person you have to meet, though."

"Trudie, the German refugee," Bernice said. "She's our new friend."

"Don't call her that anymore," Ruth said. "She's American."

"Not yet," Bernice grumbled. "She's still a refugee."

"We have a few refugees in our neighborhood, too," Shirley said. "One moved next door to your old apartment, Hannah. He was a professor at Heidelberg University, but they burned all his books. He spends half his time at the library and the other half looking for a job."

"Our refugee has a job," Debbie announced. "He's a doctor, and we made him an office."

"Ow! Ow!" Teddy shouted suddenly, falling to the ground. "Someone shot me."

"Get up," his sister said without looking at him. "I'm getting sick of your nonsense."

"But his cheek," Reva said.

"It's bleeding," Carol added.

Small blots of blood were staining the snow where Teddy lay, and Bernice gasped and grabbed him.

"Get him in the house. Call Dr. Ackermann," Ruth shouted.

Shirley bent and examined the little boy's face. "It's all right. Only a cut. Rub some snow on it."

"Next time I'll knock his head off," Arthur called from his backyard. He bent to make another iceball.

"Who's that?" Shirley whispered.

"Our local neighborhood Nazi," Hannah said. "You should hear what his father did."

Another ball came flying, toward Hannah this time, but she ducked.

"You quit saying that about my father. He's going to put you all against a wall and really shoot you," Arthur said, jumping up and down and laughing.

"He's insane," Hannah said with a shrug. "We don't pay attention to him anymore."

"It's kind of hard to ignore him, isn't it?" Shirley asked.

"It's easy to ignore him," Hannah said as loudly as she could. "He's nothing. He doesn't exist. How can we pay attention to something that doesn't exist? Ha Ha."

"Oh, yeah? Well, you should see what I have in my cellar, if you're so smart," Arthur called.

"Hannah, be careful," Shirley whispered. "He looks dangerous. My mother said to expect people like him out here in the country. She says that's how my cousins, the Shapiros, disappeared."

"Ah, he's a coward. He's afraid to move from his own backyard," Hannah said. "Come closer and say that," she shouted at Arthur. He didn't move and Hannah pulled away from Shirley and stepped toward the driveway. Somehow, it was important to show that Hazelton was perfect, and Arthur was spoiling it.

"Hannah, don't be a wise guy," Ruth called.

"Come on over here," Arthur dared, polishing an already shining iceball.

Hannah moved several steps closer. She was now on the edge of the Marshalls' property, the first time she had ever stood so close to Arthur's house.

Arthur raised his hand to throw the ball, but was stopped by a sudden rapping on the window. He turned and looked toward the house. Hannah did, too, and could see Mr. Marshall, motioning for his son to come in. She moved closer to see if Mr. Marshall was wearing a Nazi uniform.

"Get away!" he shouted, raising the window. "Off my property! Fast!"

As she backed away to leave, Arthur flung the iceball, hitting her hard in the stomach. Then he ran to the house and slammed the door behind him.

She couldn't breathe and slowly sank into the wet snow, clutching her stomach. She twisted and turned, trying to get some air, her head moving closer and closer to the Marshalls' cellar window.

"Get up, Hannah, crawl over here," her friends called.

Finally, the breathing began. "I'm O.K.," she whispered. "But my head. I think I'm seeing things." Hannah rose slowly to her feet, almost falling once again, into the arms of her friends.

"What did you see?" Ruth called. "Are you fainted?"

Hannah took a deep breath. "There's somebody in the Marshalls' cellar. I think—I think I saw Billy."

Twenty-five

HANNAH GLANCED AT THE SMALL CHRIST-mas tree next to the sergeant's desk and touched the silvery tinsel. It was softer than she had expected.

The small room was crowded, and on one of the wooden chairs that lined the wall, Mrs. Hermann sat clutching her pocketbook and nervously opening and closing the catch. Her husband, she had told the sergeant, had had to go to work, but he would come down as soon as he could.

On the chair to her left, Mrs. Marshall, wearing white gloves and a hat with a dotted veil, was crying, and Mrs. Hermann put her thin, red-chapped hand on her sleeve. "It's all right. My boy is safe. Your husband didn't hurt him," she kept repeating.

Mr. Travis leaned against the wall, sucking on an empty pipe. The noise sounded like someone who had to blow his nose. Zack, Hannah, Shirley, and Mr. Brand stood by the sergeant's desk. "You are not going down there without me," Mr. Brand had told his children.

Directly in front of the desk, Billy waited patiently. A few feet away, Mr. Marshall stood at attention, his back straight and his arms at his side. He had already caused the sergeant to scowl when he had saluted him.

"O.K., Billy, let's hear your story first," Officer Mac-

Shane said. "From the beginning, the night of the Travis girl's party."

"Boy, that seems like a long time ago," Billy said. "But I'll try." He told about the invitation that he had thought was real until Irwin and Zack met him near Lucille's and convinced him it was only a joke being played on him and Hannah. "That's Hannah over there. Hi, Hannah." He waved, and she smiled at him weakly. "Boy, that made me real mad. I mean, makin' fun of Hannah, who's a nice kid and real smart. But I didn't tell Zack how mad I was. I just said O.K. and started to go home. And him and Irwin started to go home, too. Then Hannah come runnin' up, and I seen her, and I thought, again, what a dirty trick Lucille and Cynthia was playin', and I picked up this rock and heaved it at the house. I didn't mean to break nothin', just to scare whoever was inside. That's it."

"Did you run away?" Officer MacShane asked.

"I guess so. An' when I seen that the other kids was still there, I told them to run, too. But they didn't. How come, Zack?"

Zack shrugged.

"Where did you run, Billy?"

Billy thought for a moment. "Well, I began to go home, but then I thought, gee, my folks would wonder why I was home so early. And they was real happy that I was invited to a party. I ain't never been invited before to no party, and my dad loaned me a tie and my mom ironed my old shirt so it looked real swell. So I didn't want to tell them I wasn't really invited nowhere."

Mrs. Hermann wiped her eyes and sniffed loudly.

"And then what?" the sergeant asked.

"Well, the only other friend I had was Hannah, so I

thought I would go to her house and wait and explain what I done." He turned and looked at Hannah, who moved to hide behind her father. "But they didn't come home. So I waited, and I walked back and forth between there and the Marshalls' house. Then Mr. Marshall comes out and yells at me to scram." He stood up very straight and smiled. "But I tell him it's a free country and I can walk anywhere I please."

Mr. Marshall, who had been staring straight ahead and seemed not to be listening, suddenly muttered, "Free country! Ha!"

"You'll have your turn, soon," Officer MacShane said. "And then what, Billy?"

"So then, he says to me that he seen me go to Hannah's house a lot and he seen me shoot baskets with her brother, Zack, and didn't I know it was against the rules to hang around with Jews?" He scratched his head. "I never heard of no such rules, did you?"

"Not in this country, Billy," Officer MacShane said.

"Yeah, me neither," Billy said happily. "And I says to him, what difference does it make who I hang around with? Jews is just like anybody else, and I like Hannah and Zack. Zack is the best foul shooter I ever seen."

Officer MacShane smiled. "One point for your side," he said softly. Then he cleared his throat noisily. "What else did Mr. Marshall say?"

"He said this guy, Hitler, is comin' here with an army, and we better get ready to help him. He tells me that I'm so big I could be in his army—"

"Not the army!" Mr. Marshall shouted. "His storm troopers, you idiot."

"Well, whatever," Billy said, shrugging. "Anyhow, he says that if I wanna help, I better stop bein' friendly with the Jews."

"Did you want to help?" Officer MacShane asked.

Billy laughed. "Are you kiddin'? Who would want to be in an army with Mr. Marshall?"

"But how did you get in his cellar?" the sergeant asked impatiently.

Billy moved closer to the desk and leaned on it. "Well," he whispered, "Mr. Marshall tells me he's got all these swell guns in his cellar and did I wanna see them? What the heck! Hannah and Zack didn't come, and I thought it would kill some time. So I go into his house."

"Was Mrs. Marshall there?"

"Maybe. I didn't see her."

"And did Mr. Marshall have guns?"

"Ah, a couple, but they was old, real old, and all rusty."

"Those guns were used in the Revolutionary War," Mr. Marshall shouted. "They belonged to my ancestors, who fought for this country which is now being run by —by them." He looked angrily at the Brands.

"And did you leave after that?" the sergeant asked, ignoring Mr. Marshall.

"I was just about to, and then Mr. Marshall says he sees a police car comin' up the street, and I got scared and told him what I done, and he says even though I don't want to help Hitler, he's gonna help me. He says he's gonna keep me hid in his cellar so the Jews won't get me. I tell him it ain't the Jews I'm scared of, it's the police 'cause I done somethin' bad. An' he says that the Jews run the police—"

"They do," Mr. Marshall said. "Admit it. Haven't they paid you to arrest me?"

Officer MacShane looked at Mr. Marshall and shook his head sadly. He turned to Billy. "You were there for a long time, young man. Didn't you know your parents were worried sick?"

Billy seemed surprised, and then angrily grabbed Mr. Marshall's arm. Officer MacShane stepped between them and moved them farther apart. "But he said," Billy protested, "that he was gonna tell them where I was. He promised. I even writ them a note on some of the magazines Mr. Marshall give me to read." He turned around and held out his hands to his mother. "Ma, I'm sorry. I thought you knew where I was."

"I couldn't take a chance," Mr. Marshall explained. "I was not finished with your indoctrination."

"Indoctrination?" Officer MacShane asked. "And what was that?"

Mr. Marshall began to rub his palms together. He didn't look at anyone but talked, it seemed, to the wall behind the desk. "I was instructing him in the theories of the Führer, our leader, Adolf Hitler. He was a good prospect. He would obey without question. He would help us destroy the Jewish conspiracy. They had brought in people from the Führer's own country, more Jews. I could not let that happen." The people in the room watched Mr. Marshall in silence.

Suddenly, Mrs. Marshall jumped up and screamed, "He's a sick man, officer, can't you see that?"

"Yeah, he sure is nuts," Billy mumbled.

Officer MacShane shook himself and asked softly, "Did your wife and son know you were holding Billy in your home?"

"No, they knew nothing. I kept the cellar door locked and brought him his food at night." He sighed. "He would have made a fine storm trooper."

"Wait a minute," Hannah called out. "Arthur knew. He said I should come and see what was in his cellar."

"My son thought I had ammunition down there. I had told him it was dangerous and that he was not to go into the cellar."

The sergeant sighed. "Well, Mr. Travis, do you want to press charges against William Hermann for damaging your property?"

Mr. Travis slowly tapped the bowl of his empty pipe against his palm. "No, officer. The boy has suffered enough at the hands of this—this maniac bigot."

Officer MacShane burst out laughing. "Oh, that's a good one, Mr. Travis. That remark brightened my whole day."

"What, officer?" Mr. Travis asked. "I don't understand."

"I'll give you a hint. When you go home, sit down with your daughter and ask her why she didn't invite young Hannah, here, to her party. That's what started this whole mess, you realize. I don't think you'll be surprised at her answer. It's probably something you taught her yourself. You know, Mr. Travis, there are bigots and there are bigots."

Twenty-six

ALL IN ALL, SHIRLEY'S VISIT HAD WORKED out pretty well, Hannah thought. She was even sorry that tomorrow would be her last day in Hazelton. Ice skating, meeting her friends, two movies, and an exciting day at the police station. What more could anyone want?

"I put the candles in the menorah, and I put the bowl of applesauce on the dining-room table," Shirley announced. "What else should I do?"

"Nothing. Just relax and have a good time," Mrs. Brand said, smoothing Shirley's hair. "Your friend, Hannah, is so busy upstairs making herself beautiful, you have to do all her chores."

"It makes me feel at home," Shirley said. "I don't mind. Anyway, I'm so nervous about meeting all these people, I wanted to keep busy."

"That's foolish. They're people like you and me. The Ackermanns are very nice, and they were so happy to be invited to our Hanukkah party." Mrs. Brand plumped up the pillows on the sofa and patted the backs of the chairs. "Hannah, come down already. You're keeping Shirley waiting."

Hannah jumped down every other step. "O.K., here I am. Start the festivities." She examined the dining-room table and counted the piled-up plates. "Did you remember one for Billy?" she asked.

Mrs. Brand sighed. "I remembered."

"I think it was really nice of you to ask him," Shirley said. "Now he'll be able to say he was invited to a real party."

Mrs. Brand sniffed. "It wasn't my idea, believe me. I don't know what a Gentile boy is going to do at a Hanukkah party. But Hannah insisted."

"What do you think he's going to do at a Hanukkah party?" Zack said, laughing. "He'll eat four hundred potato pancakes with applesauce, just like everyone else."

"Yes, but the Ackermanns," Mrs. Brand protested. "I don't know how they'll feel about having him here."

"How should they feel?" Hannah said. "Billy's a real hero. He fought for the Jews against the wicked tyrants."

"A regular Judah Maccabee," Mr. Brand said, laughing. "Except that Judah was Jewish himself."

"Anyway, it's not the Ackermanns you're worried about, Ma. It's you. You're the one who feels funny about having a *goy* in the house." Zack shook his finger at his mother as if she had been naughty.

"So, what can I do? You can't change at my age."

"I'll get it," Hannah called as the doorbell rang. "It's the Ackermanns."

They entered with a blast of freezing air. "Good evening," Dr. Ackermann said. "Happy Hanukkah."

There was a bustle about removing coats and hanging them in the closet. Finally, everyone sat down.

"As soon as everyone's here, we'll light the menorah," Mr. Brand said. "Ah, I hear our other guest at the door now."

"I'll get it," Hannah shouted again. "Hi, Billy. Gee, you look really nice."

"Hi, Hannah. Am I late? You said . . ." He stood near the door, shifting a carefully wrapped package from one hand to the other as he removed his jacket.

"Right on time," Mr. Brand said, shaking Billy's hand. "Welcome. Do you know the Ackermanns?" He introduced them. "Trudie, here, will be in your class when you go back to school on Monday."

Billy nodded and looked at Trudie. "Gee, you're pretty," he said.

Trudie blushed, and Hannah narrowed her eyes at her. "She's not so pretty," she mumbled.

"This is for you," Billy said, handing the package to Mrs. Brand, but not taking his eyes off Trudie. "My mother sent it over. She baked them."

Mrs. Brand examined the gift as if it held a bomb. "That's lovely. You'll thank her for me, please."

"Are they cookies? Oh, good, I'll put them on a plate," Hannah said. She pulled her mother closer. "What's the matter with you, Ma? Do you think they're poisoned?"

"Who knows what's in them? They came from a *goyishe* kitchen," Mrs. Brand whispered back.

"There are bigots and there are bigots," Hannah said, echoing Officer MacShane's words, which she had been thinking about ever since he said them. She wondered who was worse, a man like Mr. Marshall, who let people know he hated the Jews, or a man like Mr. Travis, who kept it quiet. When she had asked her father, he smiled.

"Let me put it this way," Mr. Brand had said. "If I met Mr. Marshall in a dark alley and nobody was looking, he might hit me over the head with a hammer. Later, if Mr. Travis came along, he would carefully walk around my body and say to himself, 'Why should I wrinkle my suit helping that poor Jew?' Then he would probably send flowers to my funeral, and everyone would say what a nice fellow he is."

"All right, everybody, gather around," Hannah's father was calling. "Come, Mrs. Ackermann, stand closer so you can see."

Hannah giggled. Mrs. Ackermann was a full head taller than her father and could probably see from anywhere in the room.

"Ya, *Herr* Brand, it is lovely," she said with a smile.

"Let's all sing together," Mrs. Brand said.

First, they chanted the blessings over the lights in Hebrew and then Mr. Brand, seeing Billy standing off to one side, said, "And for our young guest who may not understand, I will translate. 'Blessed art Thou, O Lord, Our God, who has commanded us to kindle the Hanukkah light. Blessed is he who performed miracles for our ancestors in those days—' "

"—and in this time, also," Dr. Ackermann added. He sighed. "It is a miracle, no? That we should be in this beautiful land, free and safe?"

"Yeah, now that the Nazi next door is in jail," Hannah said.

"Ah, he is a sick man," Mr. Brand said. "I feel sorry for him."

Hannah slapped her forehead. "Pa, how could you? He was dangerous. I hate him."

"No more!" Mr. Brand said. "We won't speak of hate tonight. It's a happy holiday, reminding us of a great Jewish victory over the Syrians."

"Gee," Billy said, "when was that, Mr. Brand? I didn't hear nothin' about a war."

Mr. Brand laughed. "It would be a miracle if you

146

did. It took place more than two thousand years ago when Judah Maccabee and a small band of Jews rose up against the Syrian conquerors and—"

"—beat them to a bloody pulp," Zack interrupted. "Boy, we could sure use old Judah today. I'll bet he'd give Hitler a run for his money."

The Ackermanns' elder daughter, Wilma, shook her head angrily. "You don't know, you just don't know. You mustn't treat Hitler as a joke. If you could see what he is doing now. He tells all the children they must spy on their parents and report whatever is said in the house. He rewards them if they say something bad about their parents, and many times the children lie. We had a maid, once, you remember, Mama? Her son told the storm troopers that she worked, once, for a Jewish family. They arrested her and dragged her off to their headquarters. They tortured her so badly that today she is insane. And her son says he was only doing his duty. So please, no jokes about Hitler."

"Wilma, dear," Dr. Ackermann said softly. "Do not think about this anymore. Zack meant no harm."

Hannah looked angrily at Wilma. What did she have to bring that stuff up for? This was supposed to be a party. "Hey, Billy, have you ever tasted latkes?" she asked, glancing at Wilma to see if she would let her change the subject.

Her mother smiled at her gratefully. "Yes, my potato pancakes. Come and eat, everybody. Billy, let me fill your plate."

"Is this the best party you ever went to, Billy?" Hannah asked.

He took a large bite of his pancake and swallowed quickly. "It sure is. Ah, Hannah, you're teasing me. It's the only party I ever went to."

Twenty-seven

"GOT EVERYTHING?" HANNAH ASKED SHIR-
ley, as they stood on the porch waiting for Mr. Brand
to warm up the car. "Gee, it was nice having you visit.
And look"—she stood back and examined her friend—
"you came out all in one piece."

Shirley laughed. "It's pretty nice out here, Hannah.
I'll tell my mother that it's not as dangerous as she
thinks. Maybe, someday, we'll move. . . . No, we'll never
move."

"But you can come often. I know. You can come for
the whole summer vacation. How's that?" Hannah
asked.

"Sure," Shirley said. She picked up the small suitcase
while Mr. Brand took the larger one. "Hey, who's that
across the street?"

"Oh, her? That's the notorious Cynthia Sherwood,
writer of fake invitations. You don't want to meet her."
Hannah stuck out her tongue.

"Yeah, but . . ." Shirley put down the suitcase and
moved to the edge of the sidewalk, peering intently at
Cynthia.

"What are you looking at?" Cynthia shouted across
the street. "Haven't you ever seen a human being before?"

Shirley moved closer, walking as if in a dream.

"Hey, Shirl, don't go any closer. You'll catch the

plague," Hannah called, but she followed Shirley toward Cynthia's.

"And we'll miss the train," Mr. Brand added.

"It's Simcha," Shirley kept muttering. "It's Simcha."

Cynthia moved back toward her house as Shirley came closer. She looked as if she had just seen a ghost. "Get away from here," she shouted. "Mom, Mom, help."

"I can't believe it," Shirley said. "If she has red hair, I'll know for sure."

"Red hair?" Hannah asked. "Look!" She reached out and pulled the hat from Cynthia's head. "Abracadabra, red hair!"

"Simcha Shapiro! What are you doing here? We thought you all were dead," Shirley shrieked.

Cynthia moved quickly toward her door, but not fast enough. Hannah grabbed her by the arm and held her.

"This is your long-lost cousin? The one who moved to the country and you never heard from again?" Hannah asked, her eyes growing wider as she spoke. "You mean this kid is Jewish?"

"Oh, my mother will be so happy." Shirley was bubbling. "When did you change your name? No wonder we couldn't find you in the phone book. We looked for years."

"Get out of here. I'm not your cousin," Cynthia said. "Our name is Sherwood."

"Is your mother home? I want to say hello." Shirley knocked hard at the door, and when it opened, she jumped up and down. "Cousin Rose, Cousin Rose, look who's here! Shirley Levine! Cousin Rose, are you all right? Hannah, call Dr. Ackermann. I think my cousin Rose is going to faint."

"She'll be all right," Dr. Ackermann said, as he came downstairs to the Sherwood living room. "That was quite a shock you gave her, Shirley. It's lucky your cousin Rose has a strong heart."

"Oh, Simcha, we have so much to talk about," Shirley said. "But I have to go home now. Maybe when I come back this summer." She bent and kissed Cynthia on the cheek.

"Blech! How can you touch her?" Hannah asked.

Cynthia sat, frozen, on the sofa. She looked neither at Hannah nor Shirley. Dr. Ackermann bent over and raised her face.

"Are you feeling well?" he asked softly. "Would you like some smelling salts?"

"She's smelly enough already," Hannah said. "Oops, I'm sorry, Shirl. I forgot she was your relative."

"Come, come, we've already missed one train," Mr. Brand said.

"O.K. So long, Simcha," Shirley called over her shoulder. "I can't wait to tell my mother about you. Let's go, Hannah. I really want to get home."

"Can you believe it?" Hannah asked her father over and over as they drove back from the station. "She had a Christmas tree and everything. I can't wait to tell Ruth and—Lucille. Ha, ha, that'll be a laugh on her. She had a Jewish kid at her party anyway."

"I know that Cynthia hasn't been very nice to you, Hannah," Mr. Brand said, "but I don't think you should go around telling everyone what the Sherwoods obviously want kept secret. If they don't want anyone to know they're Jewish, that's their business, not yours."

"Why did they do that, Pa?" Hannah asked.

"Why? Maybe they stopped believing. Maybe they were ashamed. Maybe they were afraid. You know, it takes courage to stick to your ideals and your faith when there are animals like Hitler in the world ready to kill you, and people like your friend Lucille anxious to snub you and hurt your feelings. The funny thing is that the Sherwoods were so eager to be Christians, but they didn't even know how to do that right."

"M-m-m," Hannah muttered. "Simcha Shapiro. Boy, that's hysterical."

"Remember what I'm telling you, Hannah. Don't gossip. One of the great Jewish sages once wrote, 'Put no one to open shame; misuse not thy power against any one; who can tell whether thou wilt not some day be powerless thyself?' Think about that for a while. It's good advice."

"Oh, gee whiz," Hannah said, pouting. "Can't I even tell Ma and Zack? You said we should have no more secrets in the family, remember?"

Mr. Brand sighed. "I can see that the wisdom of our ancestors is wasted on a foolish child. We'll have to sit down someday and read the Holy Law together. Now get out of the car," he said, as they pulled up in front of their house. "I have to go down to the factory for a while."

Her mother was on the phone when she entered the house.

"Get off," Hannah whispered, "I have something important to tell you."

Mrs. Brand waved at Hannah to be quiet. "Can you imagine?" she was saying. "A relative of the Levines' from the Bronx. I can't believe it."

Hannah put out her forefinger and slowly pressed down on the receiver hook.

"What are you doing? You cut me off. I was talking to Ruth's mother," Mrs. Brand said angrily.

"You were putting the Sherwoods to open shame," Hannah whispered. "That's not very Jewish of you, Ma." She smiled, knowing her father would be proud of her.

Twenty-eight

"IT'S A GHOST TOWN," BERNICE MUTTERED as she turned her pale face up to catch the warmth of the sun. "Deserted houses staring at us all around. Kind of gives me the shivers."

"This is how it was on our street in Berlin," Trudie said. "All our Jewish neighbors gone, their houses empty. I wonder who's living in our house."

"Was it pretty?" Ruth asked.

"Ah, *ya*. We had a garden, and in the summer my father would invite some friends who played in a little quartet with him. They would sit under a shade tree, and we would listen to the music. Sometimes, the birds would sing with them, which my father said was a great compliment." She smiled.

"Who did you sell it to when you left?" Hannah asked.

Trudie looked surprised. "Sell it? Hannah, they didn't let us sell it. They told us if we left the country, everything we owned belonged to the state."

"It must have been hard for you to leave all that behind," Bernice said with a sigh. "We had a garden with flowers. My mother loved that garden, and all summer long we had flowers from it on our table."

"What happened to it?" Trudie asked.

"My father covered it with bricks when my mother died. He said it was too painful to look at."

"How come he didn't do the same thing with your face?" Hannah asked. Then she gasped and pounded one fist against the other. "Oh, I'm sorry, Bernice. I forgot that I wasn't going to say such things. As the Bible teaches us, 'Do not do to others what you would not have them do to you.' "

"Boy, you sure are holy since Cynthia moved," Ruth said. "I hardly recognize you anymore."

"Yes," Hannah said, "I'm a new person."

"Let's see how long it lasts," Bernice mumbled. "I wonder where they went."

"To the Midwest," Ruth said. "My mother heard from somebody. I wonder if they'll be Jewish or Gentile."

Hannah sighed. "They will do what their hearts dictate."

"Blech, I can't stand it," Bernice mumbled, pretending to throw up. "Do you think Arthur is where his heart dictates, too?"

"Ah, poor souls. To have a crazy father in an institution. That's why they moved—to be near him."

"But their house is sold," Ruth announced. "New people will be moving in soon."

"How come you know so much?" Hannah asked. "You are the biggest nosybody gossip that ever lived."

"Uh uh, Hannah, that's not nice," Ruth said, shaking a finger. "You forgot to be holy."

"Hannah, go to your room and practice being holy!" Zack commanded, coming up the front path. "Here, catch!" He wound up for a baseball pitch and pretended to throw the ball at his sister.

"What happened to your basketball? Did you put it in the wash and shrink it?" Hannah asked.

"Little sister, you are not paying attention. The basketball season is over. It's spring, baseball time, and guess what?"

"You tried out for the team and the coach—"

"The coach said I was terrific," Zack said, rubbing his fingernails on his sweater as if to polish them. "Did you hear? I made it! I made it!" he shouted. "Let's hear it for the home team. Rah rah rah." He turned a handspring on the front lawn, and Trudie applauded.

"Thank you, fans," Zack said, bowing low. "But, please, no autographs." He bounded over their heads and slammed the front door.

"*Ya*, your brother is a nice boy," Trudie said, smiling.

"Thank you," Hannah said. "It runs in the family."

"That's what I like about you, Hannah," Ruth muttered. "You're so modest." She rose and turned to Bernice. "We'd better go. It's almost supper time. So long, Trudie. Good-bye, Saint Hannah. See you in church." She giggled and walked away.

Hannah watched them go. As they disappeared down the block, she turned to Trudie. "I don't understand them. Can't they see I'm a new and different person?"

Trudie shook her head. "No, Hannah, you'll never change. But, believe me, that's good. That's very good." And she leaned over and kissed Hannah on the cheek.